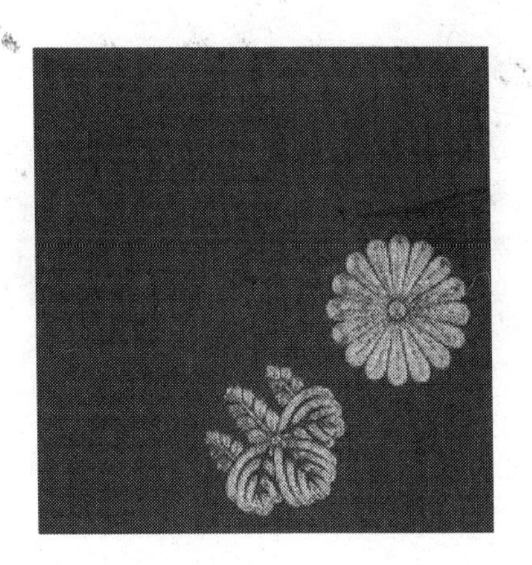

Yamato's Ghosts

A Novel by

Emmanuel Tiongco Santos

... about my novel

It's my first novel and, most likely, my last. I'm 70 years old and I'm not getting any younger. But I digress. At the outset, an elderly Asian looking man, clad in an elegant kimono is found dead at the Presidio. Two of San Francisco's finest are dispatched to the scene of the crime. They ruled out "hara-kiri" or disembowelment. There are no witnesses.

A lengthy investigation ensued, revealing the extensive and complex life of the victim, a Japanese-American, who was incarcerated in the aftermath of the attack on Pearl Harbor. It was difficult for him, his family and the Japanese-American community at large to understand why they were "locked up' while Americans of German and Italian ancestry were not. It was Pearl Harbor some argued. Others pointed to deep seated racism against Asian-Americans in general, since they first arrived in America to cut sugar cane in Hawaii and harvest crops in the Salinas valley. Naturally, these events had a profound impact on the central character and his contemporaries; albeit, in different ways.

During WWll, he joined the US Army, like so many other loyal Japanese-Americans. Trained as an agent, he infiltrated the Kempeitai, the dreaded Japanese secret police. He survived the war. Fate had once more interfered in his life, when his future bride's family managed to have him assigned to a new posting in Buenos Aires, Argentina as WWll was drawing to a close. After the war, he remained an intelligence operative, this time for the Central Intelligence Agency (CIA) in South America, to hunt down former high-ranking Nazi and Japanese war criminals escaping to Argentina.

Later in the story, the tables are turned on him when "the hunter became the hunted" by remnants of the wartime Kempeitai. These right-wing elements resolved to assassinate the victim because they believed he had betrayed them; disguising his birth, his true identity a social taboo, as cover. More importantly, they did so for the greater good of a resurgent country which was also a strong Cold War US ally in the Pacific. He was not going to become an embarrassment to a proud ancient country, causing its people to" lose face". Tragically, the CIA caved in to their twisted sense of nationalism.

Acknowledgement

... foremost, the author appreciates the extensive editing of this novel by his lovely wife of forty years, Susan Elaine Santos. Her editorial skills, gained from her life-long passion for reading fiction and a career as a public-school teacher in Fairfax County, Virginia, has made possible the completion of my work.

Umi Yukaba

If I go to sea,

I shall return a corpse awash.

If duty calls me to the mountain,

a verdant sward will be my pall.

Thus, for the sake of the emperor,

I shall not die peacefully at

home.

I - The Presidio

"Born of the sun, they travelled a short while toward the sun. And left the vivid air signed with their honour."

Stephen Spender,
The Truly Great (1932)

Long the scene of military burials and a staging point for Army campaigns and expeditions against enemies of the land, the Presidio of San Francisco has served as an almost continuously active garrison for the past 250 years.

In 1769, a Spanish expeditionary force marched from Baja California to establish presidios and missions up the coast. It was during this expedition that the great inland harbor of San Francisco Bay was discovered and plans were made by the authorities to fortify and settle the area. And so, in June of 1776, another expedition of Spanish soldiers and their families began their journey from Monterey to San Francisco. This group, under the command of Jose Joaquin Moraga, built an adobe quadrangle and living quarters and dedicated the Presidio de San Francisco on September 17,1776.

In 1821, Mexico gained its independence from Spain and included California as part of her territory. For the next thirteen years, Mexican soldiers served at the Presidio. However, the post was temporarily abandoned in 1835 when General Mariano Vallejo transferred the military headquarters north to Sonoma thus leaving the Presidio's adobe walls to slowly dissolve in the winter rains.

In 1847, American forces arrived in San Francisco during the United States' war with Mexico. The ruins of the Presidio were occupied by the New York Volunteers of the US Army who repaired several of the old buildings. In 1848, California was transferred by treaty from Mexico to the United States and the Presidio flew a new flag.

* * *

The caretaker at the Presidio cemetery opened the main gate to the public daily at 9 AM. Most of the visitors were either tourists or had family buried there. Also, for the past several years, a grey-haired, black-suited Asian man had been coming to the cemetery almost every week and leaving flowers on the grave of Ryosako Chiba. The bouquets were small and looked like the ones sold at the Marina district Safeway grocery store several blocks away in the direction of San Francisco bay.

On this particular day, Mr. Len Arenas, the caretaker was unusually late in giving his brief "welcome tour" speech to the guests. A US Senator from North Carolina had called him just as he was about to leave his office and head to the gate. He wanted to make a special videotape of his grandfather's grave. The arrangements were to be simple but time consuming. Mr.

Arenas hastily agreed to accommodate the Senator's request without sounding dismissive, as he didn't want the visitors at the main gate waiting too long either. He grabbed his keys, and like, the retired old Army sergeant that he was, he walked in quick step to his destination passing row after row of headstones. Although he has routinely given the same welcoming address for a long time, his enthusiasm has never wavered. It went as follows:

> *"When Spain decided to colonize California in 1776, it selected this area as the site for a fort or presidio to defend San Francisco Bay. More than half a century later, the discovery of gold in California naturally led to the sudden growth of San Francisco. But it was really its strategic location, a gateway to the Pacific Ocean, which prompted the U.S. government to establish a military reservation there. President Millard Fillmore established by*

executive order, the Presidio for military use in November 1850.

The Civil War in 1861 served to reinforce this notion which emphasized the military significance of San Francisco's harbor to the Union. The Spanish American War in 1898 and the Philippine-American War which ensued, from 1899 to 1902, further increased the military role of the Presidio. Thousands of troops were encamped in tent cities while awaiting shipment to the Philippines. Those soldiers who came back sick or wounded were treated at the Presidio while the dead were buried on the same grounds.

On Dec. 12, 1884, the War Department designated nine acres, including the site of the old post cemetery, as the San Francisco National Cemetery. It holds the distinction of being the first national cemetery established on the West Coast. Soldiers and sailors who died overseas serving in the Philippines, China and other areas of the Pacific Theater are interred in San Francisco National Cemetery.

There are monuments and memorials within the cemetery grounds, such as: Grand Army of the Republic Memorial (1893), the Pacific Garrison Memorial (1897), a monument to the Marines who died at the Tartar Wall in Peking, China (1900) and another to the Unknown Dead (1934). A stone wall slopes down a hill enclosing the cemetery and frames a view of the Golden Gate Bridge. Tall eucalyptus trees surrounded the cemetery. The San Francisco National Cemetery was listed as a National Historic

Landmark as part of the Presidio in 1962."

* * *

The typical San Francisco fog was unusually thick that morning and the traffic consequently worse than normal. The dense fog covered the Presidio like a pale grey mantle which a shepherd might use to protect a newborn lamb from the harsh elements. The Marin headlands across the bay were obscured from sight and the tall eucalyptus trees and Pacific cedars stood as silent sentinels lining the winding roads. Gradually the fog became wispy and dispersed towards late morning.

It was the Navy's annual "Fleet Week" celebration and the city's residents and locals in neighboring Marin and Sonoma counties were also trekking in droves across the Golden Gate Bridge to view the air shows and ships in port.

Mr. Arenas made it a point to go see the festivities every year. Although an Army combat veteran, he enjoyed swapping war stories with his Navy counterparts about the conflict in Vietnam.

The Asian gentleman patiently waited for Mr. Arenas to open the gate. However, instead of his usual somber black suit attire, he wore a ceremonial gold and green patterned kimono and carried a huge arrangement of yellow chrysanthemums. His regalia included an ancient-looking samurai sword in a worn scabbard. Understandably, the Mr. Arenas took notice and said:

> *"Good morning, Sir; you're all dressed up today. Do you have a special event to attend?"*

The kimono-clad figure bowed to him and just smiled as the gate was rolled back. He proceeded to take his usual route, a quarter of a mile through rows of headstones, some of which dated back to the Spanish American War. A slight turn downhill through a few eucalyptus trees and he was at the section for the World War II dead.

Later that same morning, as Mr. Arenas was already about performing his daily maintenance duties, the visiting US Senator, Shelby Wells, and his entourage arrived at the Presidio Cemetery gate. By that time, Mr. Arenas had also learned that the distinguished visitor was also Chairman of the powerful Senate Foreign Relations Committee and thus accorded him the assistance and protocol due his seniority in the Senate. The grave of the senator's grandfather, a Medal of Honor recipient, killed in the fighting against Filipino insurgents at Fort Santiago after the Battle of Manila Bay in May 1898, was located in the rear part of the cemetery. He was with the army contingent under the command of General Arthur MacArthur, the father of General Douglas MacArthur of World War II fame. The body of the Senator's grandfather was brought back to the United States for burial owing to his senior rank and at the request of his family whose prominence in the Army military circles dated back to the American Civil War.

* * *

The Medal of Honor was created during the American Civil War and is the highest military decoration presented by the US government to a member of its armed forces. The recipient must have distinguished themselves at the risk of their own life above and beyond the call of duty in action against an enemy of the United States It is commonly presented posthumously. The documentary was sponsored by the American Legion. It was intended to educate high school students across the country about the

Philippine-American war which lasted from 1899-1902.

The war was an armed military conflict which arose from a Filipino political struggle against U.S. occupation of the Philippines. While the conflict was officially declared over on July 4, 1902, American troops continued hostilities against remnants of the Philippine Army and other resistance groups until 1913, and some historians consider these unofficial extensions part of the war.

There are other Philippine-American War Medal of Honor recipients interred at the Presidio cemetery like: Colonel Frederick Funston, Sr., 20th Kansas Volunteer Infantry for heroism at Rio Grande de la Pampanga, Luzon, Philippine Islands on April 27, 1899. Another is Private Cornelius J. Leahy, Company A, 36th Infantry, U.S. Volunteers. His citation read: "distinguished gallantry in action in driving off a superior force and with the assistance of one comrade brought from the field of action the bodies of two troopers, one killed and the other severely wounded, this while on patrol near Porac, Pampanga, Luzon, Philippine Islands, September 3, 1899.

* * *

The conversation among the visitors had been desultory, mostly comments about the thick fog and the task of setting up the video cams for a good shoot. As the Senator, his wife, and two video cameramen were walking up the road, they noticed a green and gold clad person lying with his back to them in front of one of the graves. When they got closer, they noticed that the person was lying on his right side in front of an ornate marble headstone with most of a bouquet of yellow chrysanthemums still clutched in his left hand. The bloody sword in his right hand and his partially eviscerated body were not immediately visible until the visitors were almost at their own relative's grave.

"My God! Don't look, honey,"

the Senator exclaimed facing in the direction of his wife as he uncontrollably lost part of his breakfast.

"Oh, dear God!"

She shouted simultaneously as she realized the horrible nature of the scene. Then, she ran back in the direction of the entrance to the cemetery to find Mr. Arenas so he could call the police. She found him alone sitting at his desk in his small office filing papers. The caretaker was surprised by the sudden entrance of the Senator's wife. She was trying to catch her breath after running from the horrid scene she had just witnessed.

"What's wrong, ma'am? Are you, all right?"

Mr. Arenas was concerned by the appearance of the Senator's distraught wife. She was gasping for words, in trying to explain her behavior. He did his best to calm the distressed lady so he could find out what took place and call the authorities to report what had happened. Nothing out of the ordinary ever really occurred at this normally peaceful historical site of America's war dead.

An ambulance arrived within minutes after making the emergency call. However, the police would also be dispatched since a person was injured at the scene. For a moment, Mr. Arenas wondered if he shouldn't go to the main gate so he could show them the quickest way to the section of the cemetery where the incident occurred, or simply wait in his office in case the phone rang.

“Here ma’am, please drink this; it will make you feel better”,

he said to the senator’s wife as he finished pouring her a glass of water. This helped in calming her.

“Please wait here until I return with some help.”

He then proceeded to meet the authorities at the main gate. The police arrived shortly in a patrol car and also an unmarked police vehicle. The caretaker greeted the officers:

“I’m glad you folks got here quickly! I’m Len Arenas, cemetery caretaker. Something terrible has happened.”

He was about to describe the incident in detail when the two other officers wearing civilian clothes arrived at the scene. They identified themselves as Inspector Mac Chavez and Sergeant Jeven Lee. They asked him to lead them to the scene. Senator Wells suggested that the detectives walk and pick up his wife along the way, while he rode with the medics and took the longer vehicle path. The uniformed officers and medics agreed recognizing that time was critical.

As the caretaker and the medics drove away, Inspector Chavez went to find the Senator's wife to obtain an eyewitness account of the incident. They found her sitting in the same chair where Mr. Arenas had left her in his office only minutes ago. She was still distraught over what she had seen but had managed to regain her composure. Responding in a distinct North Carolina accent, she told the Inspector who she was and that there was no time to waste.

> *"You have to hurry, Sir! The Senator is with the wounded man; he looked awful",*

she added.

> *"Yes ma'am; we're on our way",*

replied the Inspector. While making their way to the scene, the Inspector couldn't help worrying that this matter might not remain a local one for very long either. A situation like this could get messy especially from a jurisdictional standpoint with local city officials. The Senator was still standing by the body when the officers reached the grave. His face was still pale gray giving him a monotone visage, but his emotions were under control.

The video cameramen had propped their equipment against an old oak tree.

“We’re police officers",

remarked Sgt. Lee, showing his police badge.

“Please, don’t touch anything.”

Inspector Chavez approached the grave from the right side. Not wanting to disturb the death scene, he slipped on a sanitized plastic glove which he took out from his right jacket pocket. Then carefully leaning over the flowers, he touched the neck area to determine if there was a pulse. There was none but the body still seemed to be warm even on this cold morning.

“It looks like the old man committed suicide, hari-kiri to be exact”,

his partner standing beside him quietly muttered.

"Considering the attire of the old man, it seems like a reasonable explanation for the sword, kimono, flowers, and so on."

"You could be right",

the Inspector replied.

"But you can never be sure about these things. There is no suicide note lying around, is there? If this man is Japanese, we're in for a lot of work. The Japanese have a peculiar way of often reversing the obvious. That's just the way they are; it's a cultural thing. Still, you said it though, it sure looks like hara-kiri. But I thought they

always wore white when they did this sort of thing,"

Sgt. Lee added.

The Inspector agreed that this would be the logical conclusion for now, but that something else was bothering him. He had been on the San Francisco police force for almost two decades and his instincts told him something quite different. He has seen his share of violent homicides during his career.

Not that long ago, he witnessed firsthand in next door Marin County a judge and three black militants killed. Superior Court Judge Harold Haley was murdered on that hot summer morning of August 7, 1970. George Jackson, a celebrated convict author, and two other San Quentin prison inmates were also slain as Jonathan Jackson, younger brother of the author, tried to free them. The Inspector was in the courtroom representing the San Francisco Police Department (SFPD).

He remembered how the young Jackson entered Judge Haley's courtroom wearing a long overcoat with a briefcase in hand and a paper sack, from which he produced a rifle, a sawed-off .12 gauged shotgun and a Browning .380 caliber pistol, respectively. As they made their way out of the building, they were gunned down in the parking lot by sheriff's deputies, local police officers and a squad of San Quentin guards on their way back from a nearby shooting range. Angela Davis, a former UCLA professor, was accused and later acquitted of buying the weapons that Jonathan Jackson had brought into the courtroom.

It was from the violent incident that the Inspector began to be extra suspicious of strangers wearing outfits which seemed out of place with either the locale or weather. He was thinking of the Presidio victim who seemed out of place, clad in a Japanese kimono with samurai sword and getas to boot. He turned for a moment to gaze at San Francisco Bay visible beyond the rows of headstones. Then he asked his partner to get the body to the coroner as soon as pictures and interviews had been taken.

Sgt. Lee had seen this look on the Inspector's face before, an introspective expression, a blank stare void of any emotion. He had been his partner now for ten years and they had solved a lot of homicides together. But, in all that time, the Sergeant has only seen the Inspector look like this on two other occasions and both murders remain unsolved. With the body removed, the Inspector turned his attention to the Senator. A dignified looking and well-dressed gentleman, Senator Wells was more than anxious to tell the Inspector what he had witnessed.

"My wife is obviously upset, Inspector. As you can see from the mess on the lawn, I haven't been any stronger either. I served in Korea and saw combat but it wasn't close to anything like this. Also, that was a long time ago."

"I understand, Sir",

replied the Inspector.

Almost whispering at times, the Senator told the detectives the purpose of his visit to the cemetery, the number of people in the entourage and that they were staying at the Fairmont Hotel downtown. He added that his wife's heart condition made a late morning visit more desirable since she wasn't a morning person and other small details which seemed to be irrelevant at that moment. Inspector Chavez listened carefully, his head leaning slightly to one side, his hands in his coat pockets.

"I really don't know what else to tell you, Inspector. I've probably said too much already. I'm sure that as a professional, you understand how difficult this morning has already been for my party."

The Inspector asked him a few more questions about the position of the people, who stood where, and what everyone was carrying. The second group of crime investigation scene personnel arrived to finish measurements and take samples of the soil and grasses near the headstone. The Inspector, Senator, and the video crew walked back to the caretaker's office to meet with Mrs. Wells.

She had recovered her composure, but her face was pale with shock and her hands were still gripping the glass of water Mr. Arenas had given her earlier. The Inspector said it would be all right to take her back to the hotel; he would interview her later. After getting their suite number at the Fairmont, the couple drove off in their rented black Cadillac. The two members of the video crew remained for a few minutes. They were the only employees of a video company named "Forever Views". Neither of them had ever met the Senator and his wife before that morning as the job had been arranged over the phone. The Senator had been impressed with their advertisement in the yellow pages. They were a last-minute replacement for the original crew who had eaten some bad oysters at Fisherman's Wharf the night before. They didn't have much to add to the Senator's version.

Both men did mention that the dead man's getas looked like they hadn't been worn. Considering the damp grass the man would have to have crossed, this seemed slightly incongruous. The Inspector made notes to remember to ask the caretaker later if he had noticed the shoes. The young men gave the police officers a business card and left in their van with the business logo purple on chartreuse. It looked garish but certainly got attention.

Before leaving the cemetery, both homicide officers also talked briefly to the caretaker. The Inspector asked Mr. Arenas if he had noticed if the victim had been wearing shoes when he arrived that morning.

"Well, not exactly", he replied.

"In fact, the man wore wooden shoes or clogs which made a distinct kind of scrapping noise on the pavement. They must have been part of his attire".

"Right", the Inspector said.

The dead man had been wearing getas. As a young airman stationed in northern Japan, the Inspector traveled the country. His favorite area was northern Honshu, its largest island. There, traditional ways and customs continued to be observed in Aomori prefecture and its small towns of Misawa and Hachinoe. The Japanese still routinely wore kimonos and the getas or clog shoes everyday well into the late 1960s'; something more prevalent than in the modernity of Tokyo, and other large urban centers such as Osaka.

This came about largely because there was a higher concentration of American occupation soldiers in those parts of the country. It continued for years even after the Allied occupation ended on April 28, 1952, when the terms of the Treaty of San Francisco went into effect. That agreement was signed by Japanese

Prime Minister Shigeru Yoshida and U.S. President Harry S. Truman allowing the US Armed Forces to continue their use of military bases in Japan.

The air raids on Japan's urban centers during the war left millions displaced. There were also food shortages created by bad harvests and the demands of the war. When shipments of rice and other basic provisions from neighboring Asian countries such as Korea, Taiwan, and China ceased, the situation only worsened. The repatriation of Japanese living in those countries along with hundreds of thousands of demobilized prisoners of war aggravated the problems in Japan further, as these people put more strain on already scarce resources. It is estimated that over 5.1 million Japanese returned to Japan in the fifteen months following October 1, 1945, and another million returned in 1947.

Major problems like alcohol and drug abuse, deep exhaustion, declining morale and despair developed. It became so widespread that it was labeled the "kyodatsu condition" (kyodatsujoutai or state of lethargy). Inflation was likewise rampant and many people turned to the black market for even the most basic goods.

Throughout most of post-war Japan, life was chaotic particularly in the rural areas. The personal surrender broadcast by Emperor Hirohito at the end of the war had come as a shock to the Japanese citizens. After all, they had been told for years about Japan's military might and the inevitability of victory. In the end, these beliefs were proven false. In reality, however, these were only secondary concerns since the entire nation was also facing starvation and homelessness.

In the 1950s, the Katsutori culture emerged in response to the scarcity of the previous years, emphasizing escapism, entertainment and decadence. As a result, the phrase “shikata-ga-nai”, or "nothing can be done about it," was commonly used in both Japanese and American press to encapsulate the Japanese public's resignation to the harsh conditions endured while under occupation. However, not everyone reacted the same way to the hardships of the postwar period. While some succumbed to the difficulties, many more were resilient. As the country regained its footing, they were able to bounce back as well. The occupation set new models for relationships between Japanese men and women: the western practice of *“dating”* spread, and activities such as dancing, movies and coffee were not limited to *"pan-pan girls"* and American troops anymore. In fact, they also became popular among young Japanese couples.

Japan continued to experience Westernization well into the postwar era. American music and movies became popular, spurring a generation of Japanese artists who built on both Western and Japanese influences. American soldiers returning from the occupation brought with them stories and artifacts, including a steady trickle of martial arts from the country.

* * *

The Inspector took the long way back to the precinct station, exiting the Presidio from the Arguello gate and taking 19th Avenue back to the Marina. The morning incident troubled him. He stopped at a red light near the Palace of Fine Arts to let a group of tourists in shorts and T-shirts cross the road. The day was turning to be a typical San Francisco summer afternoon. The tourists were close to turning blue from the sudden huge drop in temperature accompanying the fog which rolled in from the bay. The light was about to turn green when one of the tourists, a middle-aged man, yelled out to him:

"Hey, buddy where can a guy get a jacket or sweater around here? We're freezing our butts off".

Another added:

"We had no idea it would get this cold late in the afternoon. It was nice and warm earlier today."

"Yeah, and here we thought we were living the American dream",

his wife added in a sarcastic tone with everyone else laughing in the background.

The Inspector told them to keep heading towards the marina, a couple of blocks away, where they'll find a bunch of people hawking sweaters. As he was pulling away from the crosswalk, he couldn't help saying:

> *"They're waiting for you folks at this time of the day, every day".*

Amused by it all, he was reminded of the remark attributed to Mark Twain:

> *"That the coldest winter he ever experienced in his life was the summer he spent in San Francisco."*

The Inspector reached his office late in the afternoon as most of the support personnel were getting ready to change shifts. His office was at the end of the hall and being a corner, had two large windows. The view on one side was the squad car parking lot. The other was a large, brick building. At least he could tell when it was daylight. Some of the newer offices had no windows. The coat rack was still missing the top peg. He slung his overcoat over one arm of the small upholstered dark green sofa in front of the parking lot window. A small oriental rug covered the standard black and white square linoleum floor and gave the room a cozy look. Green curtains matched the color of the sofa; several gold-framed pictures of San Francisco covered the walls. Although there was plenty of daylight shining in, he still turned on the overhead light and closed the blinds. Sometimes he could think better without outside distractions.

He thought he could get right back to work, but what one of the tourists said earlier that afternoon at the traffic light was sort of nagging him. What on earth did that lady really mean by saying she thought that her group was living the American dream until the day turned cold and made everyone in their group miserable? What did the weather turning foul have to do with the American dream, he thought to himself? It seemed like during the 1930s right up to the aftermath of WWll, the general citizenry equated the phrase with freedom and equal opportunity.

Inspector Chavez was thinking about the writer James Truslow Adams who, in 1931 wrote in his book *"The Epic of America"* of a "dream of a land in which life should be better and richer and fuller for every man, with opportunity for each according to his ability or achievement." He also thought about Martin Luther King, who in his "I Have a Dream" speech spoke of a vision that *"was deeply rooted in the American dream"*. He was of course making referenced to the disappearance of prejudice and a rise in community spirit. Did it still mean the same thing today, in the early 1970s'? Did it still evoke the same *"can do"* attitude that Americans are known for?

Finally, he happened to glance at the wall clock and realized how late it was and that he wasn't getting any of his case load work done. He turned on the computer and started a new case file for the information. Reaching for his phone, he hit the button and listened for the messages on his voice mail. Three messages were from his immediate superior, Captain Scott. None related to the Presidio cemetery case today. The final report on the Wilfong case was due by noon tomorrow; he would have to get clearance to be late with that one. The file folder was in his gray out box. He picked up the file and grabbed his Forty-niners team coffee mug. He might as well combine two trips in one, he muttered to himself.

The coffee machine was almost empty, so he had to tip the pot forward. Several drops hit the floor and a few dampened the suede shoes he was wearing. He was still puzzled at why the Presidio corpse was wearing getas with unmarked soles. Mr. Arenas, the caretaker, emphatically said that the victim was wearing wooden clogs when he first appeared at the cemetery gate. Two doors down from the coffee room was Captain Scott's office; his secretary took the file and said the captain would be in touch.

Back at his desk, the Inspector loosened his tie, took off his shoes and took several sips of coffee. He opened the curtains to let in the evening twilight. The street lights had just come on and the fog was visible in the distance. Sitting down in his chair, he labeled the file *"Presidio Hara-Kiri"* and proceeded to type the names of the major persons in the case and their stories. All of them would have to be interviewed again and, of course, all statements had to be signed and certified. He would try to interview the participants where they lived or worked, as coming to a police station would be too intimidating for most people.

Leaning back in his chair, he reviewed his notes from earlier that day. He decided that the Department's internal data bases were just as good a place as any to begin his research. He had a long day at work so he decided to stay put. Sitting with a cup of hot coffee with lots of milk and a little sugar, he sat down at the computer. He got off to a slow start, however. It didn't surprise him how slow the response time was given that the main computer back at work usually ran overnight reports and backed up files at night. His patience was rewarded a half hour after signing on.

His screen was deluged with a myriad of articles about Hari Kiri, also known as

Seppuku. A graphic description of Seppuku as written by the Englishman, A.B. Mitford, in 1868 read as follows:

"Deliberately, with a steady hand, he took the dirk that lay before him; he looked at it wistfully, almost affectionately, for a moment, he seemed to collect his thoughts for the last time and then, stabbing himself deeply below the waist on the left-hand side, he drew the dirk slowly across the right side, and, turning it in the wound, gave a slight cut upwards.

During this sickeningly painful operation, he never moved a muscle of his face. When he drew out the dirk, he leaned forward, stretched out his neck... at that moment, the Kaishaku, who, still crouching by his side, has been keenly watching his every moment, sprang to his feet, poised his sword for a second in the air, there was a flash, a heavy, ugly thud, a crashing fall, with one blow the head had been severed from the body; Storry, Richard; The Way of the Samurai, p33."

The Inspector vividly recalled the similarity of the wounds in the murder victim along with his partner's statement that the victim looked like he had taken his own life by committing hara-kiri. For now, all he could reasonably conclude was that no one helped the Asian gentleman since his head was not severed by a second or a kaishaku-nin. Even more troubling was that there was apparently only one set of footprints on the wet grass leading to the grave.

Sergeant Lee stopped by the office briefly on his way home to check up on his partner. The autopsy would not be conducted until they had identified the corpse. Fingerprints had already been sent to the Federal Bureau of Investigation (FBI) laboratory in Washington, DC. If the deceased had been in the service or worked for the government, they would be on file.

Finally, the Inspector decided to call it a night. He saved the file, transferred the information to a disk and locked it in his safe in the lower drawer of his navy grey government issued steel desk. He grabbed his hat and overcoat, shut down his computer terminal, rinsed his coffee mug, turned off the lights, and locked the door.

II - Seppuku

"The samurai's life was like the cherry blossoms', beautiful but brief. For him, as the flower, death followed naturally, gloriously."

Japanese history dates back thousands of years. Before Japan embarked on modernization during the Meiji period in the 1860s, it was essentially a feudal nation of lords, peasants, and the samurai. During that period, Japanese society was divided into several classes similar to medieval Europe.

In 794 A.D., Kyoto was founded as its capital; to this day it remains the historic capital, having been replaced by Tokyo as the political capital. The culture residing in Kyoto at that time was known as the Heian culture. The Heians were a very refined and artistic people, paying very close attention to ceremony and formality. Their government controlled all of the country, and thus all the land. Farmers were required to give up a certain amount of their harvest to the government as a tax, except for some small estates that were exempt from tax dues. These estates were often bestowed upon government officials and important people, such as provincial governors. But with the passage of time, these estates became more independent of the central government.

Small feuds often occurred between different land owners, or daimyos. Since only twenty percent of Japanese soil was considered fertile for farming, land was obviously prized by those who owned it, and coveted by those who did not. The demand for skilled warriors increased both to defend and to conquer. This brought about the origin of the samurai who enforced the wishes of their lord daimyo and were bound to lifelong fealty.

* * *

Inspector Chavez chose to live in a small apartment on Chestnut just off Van Ness and Lombard Streets. It was only a mile away from the Presidio where the apparent hari-kiri had taken place. One of the best features of the place was the enclosed garage. A few years back, he installed a door opener. Typical of the Victorian style apartment buildings built during the 1890s in San Francisco, it had a small kitchen, a narrow hallway leading to a den and living room, and two bedrooms. One of these overlooked Chestnut and the other a small courtyard garden maintained by his next-door neighbor.

The Inspector has long been a devotee of Victorian architecture, having lived in the Bay area practically all his life. He liked its complex structure and massive embellishments which is based on the architectural style popular during the reign of Queen Victoria in England. In the United States Victorian houses were mostly built between 1850 and 1915. San Francisco Victorian architecture was influenced by cultures from all over the world.

One can see medieval Carpenter Gothics, impressive French palaces, Turkish towers, exuberant Italian architecture, and regal Queen Annes in neighborhoods all over the city. Victorian houses have always been a symbol of the taste and status of their owners. Victorian enthusiasts have also painted them in rainbow colors, thus earning their homes a popular American designation: painted ladies.

Victorian architecture is composed of a number of different styles classified on the basis of their different application of form, technique and material. Each style is unique though they are often combined. Some of the major architectural styles used in San Francisco are: Italianate, Gothic Revival, Queen Anne, Stick/Eastlake, and Second Empire, designating it as one of the most colorful cities in the world. They show the love of architects, designers and home owners for different cultures, which have been combined in many different ways to reflect a personal expression.

* * *

A widower, the Inspector found the Marina District neighborhood shops and restaurants nearby convenient. His favorite Italian hangout, O'Solo Mio, served the best pizza and lasagna as far back as he could remember. He loved the mushroom and sausage combination pizza. But recently, it changed owners and had reopened as a Tex-Mex joint. Not that the inspector didn't like Mexican food; it's just that he could get really good Tex-Mex meals anytime he wanted in the Mission district where a large concentration of the city's Mexican-American population lived.

When he felt like exercising outdoors, he would take a leisurely walk to Funston Field a few blocks away. The park was popular with the Marina residents. There were tennis courts there and a tennis backboard where he occasionally met fellow tennis players with whom he'd share a cold beer with afterwards.

Ladies closer to his age, divorced or single like him, often used the backboards too to hit some balls. He had dated a few of them over the years but nothing serious ever really developed. It wasn't easy trying to measure up everyone he met to his deceased wife. There was a city library at the park as well. There, he kept up with current events by making reading several articles each week in nationally published papers and magazines like the Washington Post, Foreign Affairs, Harvard Business Review and Fortune. He read Field and Stream magazine too because enjoyed fishing too.

The park was named after Brigadier General Frederick Funston. He was born Sept.

11, 1865, in New Carlisle, Ohio, to Edward H. Funston, a Union lieutenant in the Civil War, and Ann Funston. In 1884 he failed the admission test to the U.S. Military Academy at West Point, N.Y. He attended the University of Kansas from 1885 to 1888 but did not graduate. Landing a position as a botanical agent for the Department of Agriculture in 1891, Funston undertook expeditions to California's Death Valley, the Colorado Rockies and Alaska's Yukon River basin, collecting specimens and filing dispatches to popular magazines about his adventures. His restless nature next led him to reporting gigs and work on the Santa Fe Railroad.

As commander of the Presidio of San Francisco he became a focal point of controversy during the 1906 earthquake and devastating fire when he created firebreaks which saved much of the city. He also declared martial law and ordered all looters be shot on sight. Several years later, when he commanded the Mexican border region at the time of Pancho Villa's raid on Columbus, N.M., he directed Brig. Gen. John Pershing's to pursue the infamous Mexican revolutionary into the interior of Mexico. In 1917, he was expected to be named commander of the American Expeditionary Forces then being readied to join in World War I. But, before the announcement came on Feb. 19, 1917, Funston collapsed and died of a heart attack in San Antonio, Texas. He was 51. The command of the American Expeditionary Force (AEF) subsequently fell to Pershing.

In retrospect, there was yet another intrepid chapter to Funston's life that most of San Francisco's citizens or the general population didn't know about this talented military officer. In 1896, he was deeply moved by a speech delivered by Maj. Gen. Daniel Sickles, a Civil War veteran and former U.S. minister to Spain, vilifying Spain for its repression of the Cuban people. Consequently, Funston joined the Cuban Revolutionary Army. For the next 18 months he served with distinction in combat and ultimately attained the rank of Lieutenant Colonel.

In early 1898, the 5-foot-4-inch, 120-pound expat officer contracted malaria, and his weight dropped to an alarming 90 pounds. He was given leave to return stateside. He had almost recovered from his illness when the Spanish-American War broke out. Governor John W. Leedy of Kansas knew of the young officer's recent service in Cuba and promptly appointed him a colonel of the 20th Kansas Volunteer Infantry. When Spain sued for peace, Funston was still training with his men in San Francisco. So, the Army instead sent his unit to the Philippines to counter a brewing insurgency.

In the wake of Spain's defeat, Filipino nationalists had welcomed U.S. troops as liberators. They also asked and expected the United States government to grant the Philippines its independence. When the United States instead moved to annex the islands, large segments of the population rebelled.

The self-proclaimed president of the Philippine Republic, Emilio Aguinaldo, who had earlier led the resistance against the Spanish, now commanded the insurgency against the Americans. On Feb. 4, 1899, two days before the U.S. Senate ratified the annexation; hostilities broke out when insurgents exchanged fire with American sentries guarding the San Juan del Monte Bridge in Manila. The Filipinos claimed the incident was instigated by the Americans.

In 1901, he masterminded a desperate undertaking to quash the guerrilla insurrection in the Philippines. The 35-year-old Funston approached U.S. Army Brig. Gen. Arthur MacArthur Jr., military governor of the recently occupied country, and proposed a covert expedition to the interior of Luzon to penetrate the guerrilla hideout of Emilio Aguinaldo, commander of Filipino resistance. Funston's plan called for 81 loyal Macabebe scouts from Pampanga province to disguise themselves as insurgents and escort several U.S. officers, Funston included, posing as their prisoners.

The local citizens of the town of Macabebe claimed that the *"Macabebe Scouts"* were actually descendants of Yaqui Indians exiled by Spanish authorities from northern Mexico a century earlier. For that reason, their allegiance to the Filipino nation had always been in doubt. The ruse Funston concocted would allow the group to infiltrate Aguinaldo's camp and capture him.

Funston was not new to the conflict the U.S. government referred to as the Philippine Insurrection; indeed, he had received a Medal of Honor two years earlier while leading the 20th Kansas Volunteer Infantry Regiment as a colonel on Luzon. He was certain his plan would succeed, and he worked to convince his skeptical superior.

The news of Funston's expedition and the capture of Aguinaldo were greeted in America with celebrations almost equaling those that had greeted the news of Commodore George Dewey's victory over the Spanish fleet at Manila three years earlier. Funston was promoted to Brigadier General of the Regular Army and received a telegram from Roosevelt congratulating him on *"the crowning exploit of a career filled with cool courage, iron endurance and gallant daring."* Funston became a national hero. There is more to the story.

In the months that followed, some Americans objected to the devious manner in which the capture had been engineered. The Boston Post editorialized that:

> *"as the details have come to light, contempt and disgust have taken the place of "admiration",*

while writer Mark Twain sniped that Funston's

> *"conscience leaked out through one of his pores when he was little."*

Even the London Saturday Review weighed in, calling the capture of Aguinaldo "a gross act of treachery." The furor eventually blew over, and Funston continued his Army career. On July 4, 1902, President Theodore Roosevelt declared the insurrection over and proclaimed a general amnesty. The war had claimed 4,234 American lives with another 2,818 wounded. The insurgents had incurred at least 16,000 casualties, while some 200,000 Filipino civilians had died, mostly from disease and starvation.

* * *

Inspector's Chavez's friends might even go so far as to label him an avid fisherman. On a moment's notice, he'd grab his pole and hike to the Presidio, situate himself below the Golden Gate Bridge and throw a line out into the Pacific. The only problem with fishing in that area is there were other city residents, mostly elderly Filipino and Chinese residents who shared his passion. Fishing lines would often get all tangled when someone caught a "keeper" and others failed to reel in their lines fast enough when someone shouted "fish on". Mayhem naturally ensued, but it was all in good fun among fellow anglers. As an alternative destination, he would drive across the Golden Gate Bridge to Marin County and fish in either Sausalito or Larkspur. Sometimes, he would drive farther north on Highway 101 to Novato and fish the Bahia there for stray stripers at the lagoon. There were fewer people fishing from the shore in affluent Marin County. They had boats.

According to California government archives, Marin County was one of the original 27 counties of California, created February 18, 1850, following adoption of the California Constitution of 1849 and just months before the state was admitted to the Union. According to General Mariano Vallejo, who headed a committee in 1850, to name California's counties, the county was named for “Marin”, great chief of the tribe Licatiut".

Marin had been named Huicmuse until he was baptized as "Marin" at about age twenty. Marino was born into the Huimen people, a Coast Miwok tribe of Native Americans who inhabited the San Rafael area. The Coast Miwok Indians were hunters and gatherers whose ancestors had occupied the area for thousands of years. About 600 village sites have been identified in the county.

The English adventurer, Sir Francis Drake and the crew of the Golden Hind was thought to have landed on the Marin coast in 1579 claiming the land as Nova Albion. In 1595, Sebastian Cermeno lost his ship, the San Agustin, while exploring the Marin Coast. The Spanish explorer Vizcaino landed about twenty years after Drake in what is now called Drakes Bay. However, the first Spanish settlement in Marin was not established until 1817, when Mission San Rafael Archangel was founded partly in response to the Russian-built Fort

Ross to the north in what is now Sonoma County.

The mission was the 20th Spanish undertaking in the colonial Mexican province of Alta California. It was founded by four priests, Father Narciso Duran from Mission San Jose, Father Abella from Mission San Francisco de Asis, Father Gil y Taboada and Father Mariano Payeras, the President of the Missions, on December 14, 1817, four years before Mexico gained independence from Spain.

One of California's early pioneers was Ignacio Pacheco, who settled in what is now Marin County in 1840. He was born on 8 March 1808, the son of Bartolome Pacheco and Maria Antonia Francisca Soto. His parents had both been members of the 1776 expedition to found San Francisco Presidio, led by Capt. Juan Bautista de Anza. He is believed to have been the first county resident to plant grape vines in the region and his influence can still be seen in the names of places throughout the area.

Ignacio received a Land Grant for his services to the Mexican Government as the head of the customs house in Monterey, California. He was originally given the Agua Caliente Rancho grant in Sonoma, which he deemed *"unsuitable for agriculture"* and later exchanged it for the Rancho San Jose grant which consisted of 6,680 acres in what is now Marin County. Today, Pacheco Ranch is comprised of roughly 70 acres of the original Rancho San Jose Land Grant.

* * *

Back at his apartment, Hari-kiri or Seppuku, as the Japanese formally refer to this form of suicide by disembowelment, was weighing heavily on Inspector's Chavez's mind. He knew that he had to learn more about it to fully investigate the gruesome scene he had witnessed earlier that day at the Presidio. To ease the anxiety, it's also fair to say that he wasn't entirely unfamiliar with Japanese culture, having been stationed at Misawa AFB in northern Japan for two years as a young airman after basic training at Lackland AFB in San Antonio, Texas. Because he was just 18 year of age back then, mortality was something he really never thought about much. Without family money for college, he enlisted so he could get his GI Bill and subsequently earn a degree. He graduated from the University of California, Davis and afterwards joined the San Francisco Police Department (SFPD).

He graduated first in his police academy class. He was one of the first Asian-Americans to join the SFPD. He always felt compelled to do or be *"twice as good"* as his white counterpart in the Department. This gave him the strong incentive to succeed and he was promoted to Sergeant and then Detective very quickly. He avoided office politics and didn't really get too involved in the social life with other police officers of his rank. Part of that was due to his bachelor status; his wife was killed by a drunk driver eight years earlier. His close friends had tried over the years to fix him up with different women, but it was to no avail. The intended matches simply gave up after a while.

The Inspector had always been fascinated with the Japanese people and culture. In high school, he learned how the Japanese sought to win the loyalty of their fellow Asians by proclaiming to rid the Pacific and Asian continent of the European colonial powers prior to the outbreak of WWll. The Japanese promised to give back the conquered territories to their rightful owners through its *"Greater*

East Asia Co-Prosperity Sphere" policy. Of course; it later turned out to be mere propaganda. The names of wartime Japanese leaders such as Emperor Hirohito and General Tojo became as familiar to him as the likes of President Roosevelt, General Douglas MacArthur and Britain's Prime Minister: Winston Churchill.

As a boy, he was frequently reminded by relatives, friends and neighbors alike of the cruelty the Japanese had inflicted on their fellow Asians during the World War II. His elderly mother lived through the three-year Japanese Army occupation of the Philippines. He would chuckle whenever he remembered what his mother said to him as he departed for military duty in Japan from Travis AFB, just north of San Francisco:

> *"Son, don't you bring back home anyone of those girls".*

But his father told him:

"Don't worry, you bring home any girl you want, son".

Such tidbits of personal history only served to further his interest in the Presidio homicide case. It was almost midnight before the Inspector realized how tired he was. His preliminary research had provided him with a good start on his case. Nodding, he could barely keep his eyes open any longer. He knew he had to have a clear head for the next day, so he set the alarm for 6:15 AM and turned in.

* * *

Morning came quickly, the alarm went off as scheduled and the Inspector jump to his feet. It was unusual for him to act like this especially since he wasn't really a morning person. He was pumped up. The case was racing through his mind and he wanted to get to the coroner's office before things got too hectic there. He was about to step out of his apartment when the phone rang. It was Sgt. Lee.

"You sound like you could use a ride this morning, partner. I've known you long enough to know when you're troubled by a case."

"Thanks a lot; can't hide a damn thing from you. I'll be ready most skosh."

Even his slang included Japanese words carried over from his GI days in the military. GI is US Government slang for *"government issue"*, days. Other slang popular with his fellow airmen were *"most skosh,"* derived from *"mo skoshi desu"*, to mean soon or in a little while. But his favorite was:

> *"Choke your motor, desu yo" from "choto mate kudasai",*

which meant wait a moment please. Sergeant Lee had come to know his friend and partner well after serving together on the force for many years. He knew the Inspector would appreciate the ride and also welcome his thoughts about the case. The Sgt. arrived before the Inspector could have a second cup of coffee. Rushing out of his place he almost forgot to double lock his door and set the alarm.

> *"Even a cop's place isn't considered untouchable to burglars in the city anymore,"*

shouted his partner from his car. The Inspector unbuttoned his tweed jacket, strapped his seatbelt, turned to his partner and in good nature said:

"Anything else, mother?"

Sergeant Lee grinned.

"No Sir,"

he replied and sped towards Van Ness and Market streets where most of the city and Federal governments offices were located. He was no stranger to homicide, either. He had been with the force a long time too and, like the Inspector, he was well acquainted with Asian culture.

Sgt. Lee's great grandfather worked as a laborer on the railroad when the two ends of the continent were being linked a century ago and helped lay tracks and blow up tunnels. The harsh treatment of Chinese laborers and other non-white immigrants by track foremen and the greedy railroad barons of that era was something that was not forgotten in a single generation. Chinese Americans have a long memory; it took a long time before they accepted American values. Ironically, it's interesting to note though that during the same period, it was rumored that wealthy families from China invested huge sums of money into the building of the American intercontinental railway.

All in all, Chinese and other Americans of Asian ancestry were not allowed to assimilate into California society until well into the 20th century. Many of the Sergeant's boyhood classmates were of Japanese descent and he learned about their culture very early in his life. At the outbreak of World War II, when Japanese-Americans were interred in camps, the father of one his grade school classmates committed seppuku out of shame and disappointment for his adopted country. He never forgot the incident; it made a lasting impression on him.

The morgue was located in the basement of one of the municipal buildings not far from the Civic Center. The head coroner, Dr. Len Veluz, was on vacation. His assistant, Dr. Ramon Centeno was filling in for him. He is an excellent administrator, but inclined to skimp on sharing information in any detail.

Actually, the autopsy had been done by Dr. Ofelia Sese. Inspector Chavez did not know her, but Sgt. Lee had talked to her on several occasions. She was dating his younger brother, Conner. Dr. Sese was in her office busy with the paper work when the officers arrived. Her curly dark hair was pulled back in a Chinese bun. She had completed the autopsy less than an hour before. She invited the officers in and after the introductions were over, got right down to business. Sgt. Lee asked her to relate the relevant details; they could read the entire report later.

"Most of the results were negative,"

the doctor said. She continued to say that the blood work showed a minuscule amount of alcohol. Probably the deceased had a drink during the last twelve hours. The stomach was empty so the person had not eaten during the same time period. The victim had lost half the blood in his body as the short sword had cut through a major artery. The coronary arteries appeared to be plugged and had the person not died, a major heart attack was certainly a distinct possibility in the not too distant future. Inspector Chavez briefly interrupted her:

"Was there anything unusual or inconsistent in your examination of the victim?"

Dr. Sese paused and took her eyes off the two gentlemen. As she tried to cross her arms while at the same time clasping her notepad, she added:

"There were several odd things that I find a little difficult to explain just now. Although, I said that the cause of death was apparent exsanguination, there was cyanosis of the nail beds and lips and a long sharp slice on the back of the neck.

Also, even though the rest of the body was clean, the deceased's feet were dirty, after the shoes and socks were removed. They were also covered with mud and small bits of freshly mown grass. The toxicology studies will take at least two weeks but poison is a possibility. The cut on the back of the neck had been administered with a long, thin blade of some type. There had been practically no bleeding from this wound. I can't make any conclusions until the rest of the blood work and toxicology studies are done."

With eyebrows slightly raised and his right hand clasping his chin, the Inspector replied in a low tone:

"Thank you for your time, Doctor."

In turn, Sgt. Lee asked her to call them when the rest of the autopsy results were in. The next stop was the evidence room to look at the clothes and other belongings of the deceased. After this, they would contact the FBI to see if a fingerprint match had been made. The officers also looked at the crime scene photos. But it was Sgt. Lee who noticed that the kimono was wrapped right over left; in Japanese culture this was the way a dead body was dressed. The living always wrapped left over right. It was just another small detail that made the case so intriguing.

The fingerprints had already been mailed to the FBI and a priority request was made owing to the possible international nature of the crime, not to mention testimony from the powerful and influential Senator Wells. Sergeant Lee was subtle in reminding the Inspector that the Senator was also Chairman of the Senate Foreign Relations Committee. He wasted no time either in getting in touch with an old friend who taught Japanese history at San Francisco State. He thought that by sharing some of the evidence gathered thus far, he and the Inspector might get a head start on the case.

Inspector Chavez looked forward to meeting Professor Michael Yonemoto at the college cafeteria. The professor was a tall Sansei, third generation Japanese-American, whose heritage was blended with an American fascination for pepperoni pizza. The Inspector ate one piece and proceeded to give the professor a brief rundown of the facts involved in the case. After the professor had finished three pieces of pizza, he held up his hand and said:

"I need more time to think this through; it is a rather complex situation. I'm usually not this cautious about giving my opinion, but I have to digest all of the facts first. Perhaps, I can be of more help if I saw the body right away. Is that agreeable with you?"

"Certainly, sounds like a good idea to me. Let's all go together now",

replied the inspector.

It took longer than the normal 20 minutes to drive from the SF State campus to the morgue at the civic center. A bicycle marathon had snarled Friday traffic into knots. The Inspector apologized for the delay. They noticed a little irritation in the professor's body language while seated in the back seat of their police vehicle. The two detectives had grown used to long waits. Having been on countless numbers of stake outs together, they had become immune to sitting for hours at a time inside their car.

The professor wrinkled his nose as soon as they entered the autopsy room. The body had been removed from the storage slab and placed on a clean table so the professor could examine it more easily.

"No matter how much disinfectant they use, all morgues smell the same",

he commented.

Sergeant Lee uncovered the face of the body first. The professor stepped up and leaned over until he was just a few inches from the dead man's nose. He quickly examined the hair, eyelids, and ears. The mouth was more difficult and he asked for a penlight.

"He's not full Japanese, you know."

"What do you mean, how can you tell that"

Sergeant Lee asked?

Uncovering the rest of the body, the professor pointed out the features that were so obvious to him but not to the police officers.

"His hair is too curly, almost kinky in the under layer. It looks like he combed in some styling goop to make it look straighter. He's way too tall for a Japanese of his apparent age. What is he, about 65-70? His skin tone is too fair, his teeth are in pretty good shape and the fillings in the back molars are old and are definitely American dental work.

The epicanthic fold at the corner of the eyes is not as distinct as in full blooded Asians. The eye color is a lighter brown and the size of the eyes is larger than that of someone who is full Japanese. There are other things that only my anthropologist buddies and I would consider important. This guy is part Caucasian. I'm sorry, Inspector. Do you have any questions?"

Inspector Chavez and Sergeant Lee raised their eyebrows at this news; another awkward piece in an evolving puzzle. Unknown to the two present detectives until then, the autopsy results were also of great interest to the professor because his avocation was forensic anthropology, specializing in ancient peoples like the Ainu of northern Japan.

"Bear with me for a minute and let me tell you a bit about the Ainu people of Japan",

the professor said.

"Full-blooded Ainu, compared to people of Japanese descent, often have lighter skin and more body hair. Ainu men have abundant wavy hair and often have long beards. The book of "Ainu life and legends" by author Kyōsuke Kindaichi,

published by the Japanese Tourist Board in 1942, contains the physical description of Ainu: 'Many have wavy hair, but some straight black hair. Very few of them have wavy brownish hair.

Their skin is generally reported to be light brown. But this is due to the fact that they labor on the sea and in briny winds all day. Old people who have long desisted from their outdoor work are often found to be as white as western men.

The Ainu have broad faces, beetling eyebrows, and large sunken eyes, which are generally horizontal and of the so-called European type. Eyes of the Mongolian type are hardly found among them. Never shaving after a certain age, the men had full beards and moustaches. The women tattooed their mouths, and sometimes the forearms."

The professor looked at his watch and added:

"I have an appointment across the city in 30 minutes but there is just one more thing that's significant. There are faint numbers in the victim's sparse gray underarm hair, five numbers in all, I think. The Japanese secret police, the Kempeitai, used to tattoo their operatives during the war in a similar fashion."

After the professor left, Sgt. Lee looked at the Inspector and commented:

"Now what does that mean? Was this guy a WWII spy?"

The three men walked from the morgue to a coffee shop next door to continue their discussion. The professor promised to stay in touch. As it was already Friday evening, the Inspector drove straight home, not expecting anything major to develop until the following Monday, when the witnesses would be interviewed again. The door to his condo had barely shut close when he found himself reaching inside the refrigerator for a cold beer, turning on the television and taking an early evening nap to King Kong attacking New York City.

* * *

The Inspector spent the rest of the weekend at the city zoo. The King Kong movie he watched on TV after getting back from the milonga Sunday morning must have sparked his interest in great apes. The day was cool and the crowds sparse. The gorillas were doing their best to ignore the humans who watched them. One kept raising his arm in an apparently threatening gesture. The gorilla's armpit was hairy, triggering the Inspector to remember the Presidio victim again. Did it have something to do about the armpit of the dead person found just days ago? As a professional, he often found it difficult to leave his work at the office. That is why he enjoyed fishing and dancing; they were activities which helped him to relax and forget about his job.

Night or day, Inspector Chavez always placed duty above all else. Whenever an idea or solution to a case came to mind, he tended to the problem right way. It was his nature to get things done on the spot and not delay fixing something which could be completed sooner. It didn't always work, but more often than not this trait has served him so well in the past. But something was still gnawing at him that weekend, so he decided to go to the morgue and take another look at the victim's body. Fortunately, Nora, the young female attendant at the morgue knew the Inspector by reputation and didn't mind his unscheduled visit. She had a crush on him ever since she was an intern with the department. Naturally, she was delighted to have his company that Sunday afternoon.

The Inspector asked Nora for a magnifying glass. He raised the victim's right arm and looked at the sparse gray underarm hair. He could see faint numbers through the hairs. He remembered reading a book several years ago, where WWII Japanese spies were tattooed in their armpits. While this was an interesting development, it only added to the mystery of the victim's identity. A break in the case was only wishful thinking at this early stage of the investigation. However, something like this, no matter how insignificant it may seem, can only help to move the investigation in the right direction.

The past couple of days since the murder at the Presidio had been stressful to say the least. Opinions from the other officers and the crime lab staff who were also present at the scene had to be considered too in order to avoid making any hasty conclusions. The weekend was over before he knew it.

III - Privileged Class

"Order exists because a system of beliefs and sentiments held by members of a society sets limits to what those members can do."

The Moral Sense, James Q. Wilson

Samurai protected their daimyos. From that feudal structure has emerged the zaibatsu structure, in which the samurai are industrial corporations clustered around financial daimyo, usually a bank or an insurance company, that owns a significant equity stake in each." According to legend, Emperor Keiko was the first Japanese emperor to retain the title of shogun, meaning a general who subdues barbarians. It is commonly believed however, that the future samurai warrior was modeled after his son, Prince Yamato.

Ironically, the samurai themselves began as horseback riding barbarians, but as time evolved, they took on an increasingly important role in Japanese society. At their peak, they were considered a caste of nobility and thus greatly influenced Japanese history and culture, particularly through their sense of honor. Seppuku, the ultimate expression of honor and integrity, was carried even into modern times, as with World War II pilots known as kamikazes. While the vision of an armor suited man carrying two swords may convincingly convey the image of a military warrior, the samurai became much more than this. Ultimately, the samurai became a way of life and death.

* * *

Morning came quickly so it seemed. The Inspector must have slept straight through the night, not remembering even dreaming about the horrid events of the past several days. A consummate professional, he often dreamt about his work. A strong cup of coffee with the Saturday paper plus a couple of aspirins to soothe his arthritis would take up most the rest of the morning. Later in the day, after picking up his dry cleaning from the laundry and a few items of groceries, he thought about going to his weekly tango and milonga classes.

He had always enjoyed dancing. He often wondered from which set of grandparents he inherited the trait. His mother had told him stories of how much his grandfather loved music and dancing. Yet, he couldn't remember ever seeing his parents dance at home. Oh, his father would shuffle his feet here and there before holiday dinner guests, but his mother could never seem to shake off those outdated Victorian values of the late 19th century. She would respond to his father's flirtatious moves saying:

"Stop it, can't you see, I'm cooking!"

The Inspector discovered his passion for tango years earlier during a golfing trip to Argentina with his Japanese buddy, Sawa San, from Kyoto, Japan. They met on a golf course over a decade ago in Maryland together with Fukuyama San, who taught them to play the game. But he died young when he was only fifty years old and missed the whole tango episode. Sawa San was a senior economist at the International Monetary Fund (IMF) in Washington D.C. while Fukuyama San was the senior representative for the Mitsubishi Corporation.

Before he got into Tango, he was content to jitterbug and fox trot his way at different dance venues in the city. It helped him in his grieving of his wife's untimely passing. It also kept him stay in shape as he never really enjoyed working out at the local YMCA. He found exercising on the treadmill boring. He would swim a few laps now and then, however; because, he liked the full workout gained from swimming. He also enjoyed relaxing in the sauna afterwards. At the end of his workout, he would often let the staff know how much better he felt although, he didn't *"look any better"*, eliciting heartfelt laughter from them.

Women of all persuasion loved dancing with the Inspector; he had great rhythm. But he never expected more from his partners; he simply enjoyed dancing, particularly Tango, for what it was. It bothered him when his partners wrongly interpreted his moves. One of the things that annoyed him about American women is that they often misinterpreted his close tango embrace as affection for them. In this respect, he admired Argentine women - those Portenas from Buenos Aires - who draped themselves over their tango partners and thought nothing of it. For them, Tango was simply a dance, a collection of emotionally filled moments, drawn out by the lyrics and rhythm of the tango itself, captured in an intimate embrace while the music played.

Well, Saturday night couldn't come soon enough and the Inspector found himself among his tango friends again. That evening, he went to one of his favorite milongas in the city's popular Mission district, with its reputation as a destination for hot Latin dance venues.

Originally known as *"the Mission lands"*, San Francisco's Mission District is named for the domains that belonged to the sixth Alta California mission, Mission San Francisco de Asis. Prior to the arrival of Spanish missionaries, much of the San Francisco Bay area was inhabited by the Ohlone people. When the Spanish missionaries arrived during the late 18th century, they found these people living in two villages on Mission Creek. It was there that a Spanish priest named Father Francisco Palóu founded Mission San Francisco de Asis on June 29, 1776.

The Mission sought to convert the local Ohlone people to Christianity. Ranchos owned by Spanish-Mexican families such as the Valenciano, Guerrero, Dolores, Bernal, Noé and De Haro were settled in the area. They were separated from the town of Yerba Buena which was later renamed San Francisco, for the Saint to whom the old mission was dedicated.

During California's early statehood period, in the 19th and 20th century, large numbers of Irish and German immigrant workers took over the place. Development and settlement intensified after the 1906 earthquake, as many displaced businesses and residents moved in making Mission street, a major commercial thoroughfare. During the 1940-1960s, it was the Mexican immigrants' turn, initiating *"white flight"*, giving the Mission District its heavily Latino character today.

The tango venue itself, *"El Rincon"* was not an upscale joint by any stretch of the imagination, but it had a nice spacious dance floor. There was a big crowd that night since there was live music and a tango exhibition by Marcelo and Romina, professional tango dancers from Argentina. They taught classes throughout the Bay area. Marcelo had greatly influenced the Inspector's style of tango: a posture with slightly bent knees as if sitting on the edge of a barrel. But the closing step was his favorite move.

It goes like this: he steps off with the left foot, then makes a side step with his right, followed by a step *"in place"* with the left foot, and then brings back the right foot together with the left. The Inspector loved this unique closing tango step sequence taught by Marcelo. He had never seen any other tango instructor do it either in San Francisco or in Buenos Aires during one of his trips there. He thought that the reason could be that Marcelo was from Rosario, another vibrant city in Argentina. He may have picked up the movement there instead of in Buenos Aires.

* * *

It was Monday morning and the Inspector was back at pounding the pavement. He had planned to make an appointment with the Japanese consulate that week. But he decided to wait longer upon realizing that the victim's identity was not going to be known anytime soon. More research and interviews have to be conducted before he can even begin to think about involving the Japanese embassy staff in the entire matter. He also thought that it might be the right time to focus part of the investigation on the person who was buried at the grave site where the victim was found. He completed his internal department report and sent it to his superiors that same day.

From the outset, everyone in the office who was involved or had any knowledge of the investigation suspected that there had to be a connection between the grave site and the victim. After all, there were more than a handful of veterans of Japanese ancestry from all past US wars buried at the Presidio. Another factor to consider was that many of the Japanese Americans who served in WWII were either from Hawaii or Southern California. They were understandably laid to rest in national cemeteries nearer their homes. So, what was the significance of the particular grave site where the slain man was found. The Inspector naturally wanted to know more about the person interred at the gravesite of Private First Class (PFC) Ryosaku Chiba, also a WWll veteran who was killed in Italy. The victim was visiting his grave the day he was found dead at the scene.

The Inspector put the word out and a day later, he got a tip from a rookie cop in the department to contact Mr. Arenas, the Presidio cemetery caretaker he had already met the previous week. Mr. Arenas just happened to also double as a historian at the Presidio Museum. And so, instead of waiting for weeks to hear back from the Defense Department about the person interred at the crime scene, Inspector Chavez and Sergeant Lee decided to move forward with the investigation by directly meeting with the caretaker.

San Francisco's political elite had branded Mr. Arenas a nonconformist. So, did his wealthy and influential family because he chose to make the military a career instead of politics or commerce. Mr. Arenas could have joined his family's successful restaurant business too. But he chose a different path. A Green Beret in Vietnam, he was awarded the Silver Star for bravery saving men in his platoon while under heavy enemy fire. He also received a Purple Heart because he wounded in combat.

Mr. Arenas's lifelong interest in U.S. military history and tradition only served to further arouse his curiosity upon learning of the Asian gentleman’s manner of death. He took the initiative to look for the cemetery file of PFC. Chiba and promptly shared its contents with the Inspector and his partner, when they arrived at the Presidio Museum.

It was another beautiful day in the city. It was almost noon and the morning fog had cleared like clockwork by the time the two detectives completed their interview with Mr. Arenas. There wasn’t much else he could tell them about PFC. Chiba, other than what the cemetery records showed. He did say, however, that he had regularly seen the victim at the cemetery on more than one occasion in the recent past. He usually came alone during the weekdays and always brought flowers. It could be that he preferred solitude over the company of throngs of visitors and tourists on weekends and holidays. The Inspector nodded his head in approval and promptly thanked Mr. Arenas for his time.

On the way back to their unmarked police vehicle, the Inspector looked up to the blue clear sky, turned to his partner and muttered: *"another shitty day in paradise"*, an expression he borrowed from an old acquaintance in Brisbane, Australia. Having known his partner for a long time, Sgt. Lee knew that the Inspector was pleased with the outcome of the meeting. It was his manly or *"macho"* way of saying that it's been a productive day.

* * *

Back at police HQ later that day, the pair got their first concrete lead. Midori Chiba, the wife of the man buried at the murder site, was still alive. She was living in a small two-bedroom apartment on Powell Street near Union Square. Excited, the two men dashed to her residence hopping on board the first trolley car in sight.

Frail but still alert, an elderly woman invited the two detectives inside her modest apartment. Her granddaughter, Kumiko, served the guests hot green tea and peanut butter cookies. She remained in the room to make sure there was no miscommunication between them. Although her grandmother had been living in the States since for a long time, she still didn't feel entirely at ease speaking in English.

Before the Inspector and Sgt. Lee actually began questioning Mrs. Chiba, they first attempted to make polite conversation. This was important given the cultural background of their host. In polite Japanese society, one is expected to answer questions directly. The Inspector also occasionally remind friends and associates, that when interviewing someone for the first time you are mindful that:

> *"In real life, you never get a second chance to make a first good impression."*

Sgt. Lee quickly made these observations of the apartment's decor. Pale watercolor seascapes hung on two walls; no boats, just water and beach. Low and comfortable looking upholstered furniture in pale gold was arranged around an ebony coffee table. A bonsai tree in an earthenware pot occupied the center of the table. The facing fireplace supported a large gold leaf mirror and an Inari plate. Bookcases filled with small samurai sculptures and art books occupied one side of the room. A small black and white cat was sleeping soundly on the faded Oriental rug by the coffee table.

The Inspector's eyes though were immediately drawn to the Japanese sword on the hallway table. The elderly widow told him that it belonged to her husband's great grandfather. It was given to him by the Japanese government for his loyal service to the Emperor Meiji as a palace guard in the 1860s'. Her husband told her that swords in Japan were relegated to museums and private collections in the modern period, when the Meiji government banned their wearing after the Restoration of 1868. However, WWll brought swords back in fashion to serve the Japanese military as a symbol of the Bushido code or *"the way of the warrior"* and its Confucian-based ethic. Prior to the Meiji period, the wearing of the sword was a class privilege restricted to the samurai class and forbidden to merchants and farmers. The true samurai revered a good sword and superior blades were passed down from generation to generation as treasured heirlooms.

The granddaughter motioned the two men to take their seats and proceeded to pour tea. She explained that they could be more direct with her as she was born and raised in the United States and not bound by tradition from the old country. She made no reservations about stating that her grandmother was naturally concerned about the nature of the visit; however, they would like very much to help them in any way they can.

Inspector Chavez inquired:

> *"What part of Japan was your husband from and when did he come to*

this country? More importantly, why did he leave Japan? We understand your position and we apologize for the intrusion. Anything you can remember will help us in our investigation."

Mrs. Chiba replied:

"My husband was born in Japan just after the turn of the century. His family came from the city of Morioka in the northeastern part of Honshu. They belonged to the samurai class. They were not wealthy but they owned a small parcel of rice land which was given to his great grandfather by Emperor Meiji.

The northeastern part of Honshu, also known as the Tohoku region, is like most of Japan, hilly or mountainous. Tohoku was traditionally considered the granary of Japan because it supplied Sendai and the Tokyo-Yokohama market with rice and other farm commodities. The climate, however, is harsher than in other parts of Honshu and permits only one crop a year on paddy land."

The Inspector asked:

"Why did he leave Japan?"

Mrs. Chiba politely nodded as if to plead with the Inspector to be patient. She hasn't had any reason in a long time to give such matters much thought at all. Her husband was a very private man and it took a lifelong marriage to learn about his past, much less recollect them during an unscheduled interview.

"My husband's father was a veteran of the Sino-Japanese war of 1894. He had seen the horrors of war firsthand as a medic in the infantry. As a young boy,

his father instilled in him the value of human life. So, he grew up obsessed with the idea of someday saving lives like his father. But there were political and economic factors that also contributed to his interest in someday becoming a physician.

The region of Japan in which his family had lived for over a century was primarily agricultural. Young men who wanted to pursue careers outside the farm such as government or commerce were compelled to go south to Tokyo or Osaka where those institutions flourished. Just getting accepted into medical school was a challenge for someone like him from the country.

Most of his classmates didn't have to face the same problem because they could afford preparatory schools or had family connections. But he persevered. He would have completed his studies if political conditions in the country hadn't changed and by the resulting war."

She faltered a bit at the last words. Sgt. Lee politely interrupted her and inquired if she felt all right.

"I'm fine, Sir; but, thank you for asking", she replied.

"It was during that tumultuous period, both economically and politically, before the outbreak of war with America that my husband decided to leave Japan like so many of his countrymen. His own father had felt betrayed by the nation he and his ancestors had dutifully served as members of the samurai class.

My husband felt little sympathy towards the extreme nationalists who were poised to destroy the legacy of the Meiji era. The influence of the political parties steadily declined and a worldwide recession loomed on the horizon. With the Diet's legislative functions reduced to little more than those of a rubber stamp, there could be no parliamentary obstruction to the tide of events that finally led to the outbreak of the Pacific War in 1941.

Starting all over in America was not easy either. With a limited knowledge of English and literally no outside means of support, my husband went to stay with relatives in the central valley.

Salinas seemed a distant place at that time when it took nearly three weeks to cross the Pacific by ship from Japan. Still, he was grateful he had at least a roof over his head and food on the table. His relatives in the valley came to Salinas from Japan by way of Hawaii. The matron of the house was his aunt on his mother's side. They were farmers and had experienced hardship all their lives. They were content living in America where its citizens had more civil freedoms although it was not always applied equally to all groups."

The last comment by Mrs. Chiba struck a chord in everyone present in the room. Everyone had shifted body positions slightly; their attention heightened by the significance and impact that such a statement had upon American society in general in recent years. The Inspector and his partner were impressed by Mrs. Chiba's grasp of the historic events of her time.

Inspector Chavez recalled the story his father had told him about the time he was told to go towards the rear of the bus as it was crossing the Potomac River from Washington D.C. into northern Virginia. It was during the early 1930s and he was going home together with his roommates, who were also his countrymen from the Philippines. Being brown or darker in skin color, he said they hovered around the middle of the bus, to comply to the other popular notion of the times that:

> *"If you're black, stay back; if you're yellow, stay mellow; if you're brown, stay around."*

Although the Inspector and Sgt. Lee had found the mother and daughter to be very cordial and most helpful, they thought it prudent to interrupt Mrs. Chiba once more. She was about to continue narrating her husband's life in the Salinas valley. The detectives excused themselves realizing that they had already been with their host for over an hour. They did not want to overstay their welcome.

Also, Sgt. Lee had started sneezing as the family cat woke up and came over to say hello to him. After thanking the host for seeing them on short notice and taking leave, they asked their host if they could return to ask more questions as the investigation progressed.

Mrs. Chiba naturally agreed and invited the detectives back. She was impressed by the professional courtesy of the two men. Despite her age and frail appearance, she still had all of her mental capacities intact. She studied to be a teacher in Japan where she acquired her skill in effectively listening to others whose opinions and beliefs may differ from hers. Later in life, she applied and honed those same skills in communities in her adopted country.

* * *

Inspector Chavez and Sgt. Lee decided to leisurely stroll through Union square to recall details of their meeting with Mrs. Chiba and her daughter. The Inspector enjoyed its sights and sounds. To him, it is one of the more colorful areas of the city, particularly during the sixties when the flower children and the Hara-Krishna sect hung out there. But it was the tall obelisk-like structure at its center that took on an added personal significance.

The monument was erected to commemorate Admiral George Dewey's victory at Manila Bay on May 1, 1898 at the outbreak of the Spanish-American War. It often crossed his mind that his father would have never immigrated to America in 1929 if that conflict had not taken place. In other words, the ensuing American military conquest of the Philippine Islands from 1899 until 1902 and its designation as a territory of the United States sealed his family's fate.

To the city's residents, Union Square is to San Francisco what Constitution square is to Athens, Trafalgar square to London and Rockefeller Center's ice rink to Manhattan. Besides being the central park of the town, Union Square is where the action is, whether for cable car bell-ringing contests or outdoor art festivals. During the Christmas-Hanukkah season, it's where crowds go to see holiday lights and colorful shop windows. It is a major tourist destination and where demonstrators also go to protest. John Geary, San Francisco's first mayor gave the land to the city in 1850, the Gold Rush year. The park saw many pro-Union rallies during the Civil War era of the 1860s, that it got the name Union square.

As the two officers crossed Powell Street after cutting through the park, Sgt. Lee turned to his boss:

"So, where do we go from here? Do you want to check out Mrs. Chiba's story about her husband's friends? They aren't that many left alive you know. They're all getting up there in age too, just like you and me."

Inspector Chavez chuckled.

"Speak for yourself, buddy. I intend to live forever."

Both men laughed loudly. Then, the Inspector added:

"I think we should focus on Mr. Chiba for the time being. We know he was a

veteran, so why don't we go to the VA and see if we can get a copy of his military file. We may find something there that may connect him to the victim. We'll have to check his medical connection too. The doctor was older than the victim, who might have been a patient."

The Inspector sounded exasperated just thinking about the enormous task ahead of them:

"We may both be a lot older before this mystery gets solved. Don't forget that the records in many of the older civilian hospitals get pitched after a few years. At least the military holds on to everything. We really need to get back to the office now. It looks like our nice, sunny day is going to pour on us."

No sooner were the words spoken that it began to sprinkle. That's when Sgt. Lee informed the Inspector that he has already contacted the VA. It is putting together Mr. Chiba's military file and that they'll send it over as soon as they get done copying its contents. A clerk had told him that the Veterans Administration (VA) was in the midst of completing a major project, copying and storing the records at a new facility for veterans dating back to the First World War.

The Inspector replied:

> *"When it rains, it pours; we'll probably get the VA file at the same time the fingerprint results from the FBI come in. We're going to have to burn some midnight oil to get through all the data to keep the Chief off our backs."*

"Yeah, I know, what you mean", said Sgt. Lee.

* * *

Back at the office, the Inspector received several phone calls not related at all to the Presidio case. These had to be returned. Although, he would have preferred solving one case at a time, it simply wasn't the practical thing to do. Staffing shortage was a persistent problem in the department and the priority of a case could change any time.

With the case workload delegated and out of the way, Inspector Chavez was again free to look over his notes on the Presidio case. And sometimes, even a fresh set of new eyes could reveal clues unseen before. He thought about asking his partner to come over and help out, but changed his mind. Maybe a cup of coffee would wake his tired brain, he thought. After drinking half a cup, he leaned back in his chair and closed his eyes to visualize the crime scene once more.

What was it about the shoes? Why did the caretaker insist that the dead man had been wearing getas? Was there a connection between the victim and the person in the grave? The chair gave a lurch as the Inspector almost fell out when the phone rang and woke him up. It was to Dr. Ofelia Sese, the assistant pathologist:

"Several days before, the body of a homeless man had been found near the intersection of Clement Street and 19th Avenue. Forensics had already done an on-site inspection and gathered all the available evidence before the heavy rains came.

The victim is also Asian, between 60-70 years of age, and had died of an apparent stab wound to the stomach. The rains had washed the blood conveniently down the nearest storm drain. Normally, I wouldn't have bothered you about a case like this, but after discovering five numbers tattooed underneath the victim's left armpit, I thought you should know about it.

Just like the Presidio body, the numbers were hidden in the hair. But, although the body found on Clement Street was very unclean, the clumped, greasy hair had separated enough to reveal the numbers. I took the liberty of asking your co-workers to run the prints to find out if he's in the system. If he is, we will have an ID soon."

"That could be relevant; you did the right thing, Doctor. There could be a connection to the Presidio case. We can't afford to overlook anything right now given the high profile this case, and before any information leaks to the media. We'll get back to you soon. Thank you, Doctor; I owe you one,"

replied the Inspector.

Dr. Sese was most helpful that day. She not only alerted the two detectives about the homeless corpse with tattooed numbers similar to those found on the Presidio victim, but also reminded them of something quite obvious. When people are assigned numbers, it's usually because they are counted as part of some group, just like members of the Armed Forces who are assigned serial numbers or civilians given social security numbers.

* * *

Back in his apartment that evening, the Inspector thought about the group association that Dr. Sese made referenced to with regard to the two dead Asian men. He believed that a society that tolerates significant antisocial behavior can't survive in the long run. However, most scholars argue that Japan is a society that relies on social rather than ideological sanctions. The social restrictions they placed on their citizens are meant for the greater good of its populace because they emphasize the benefits of harmony. In fact, Japanese children learn from their earliest days that human fulfillment comes from close harmonious association with others. Children learn early to recognize that they are part of an interdependent society, beginning in the family and later extending to larger groups such as neighborhood, school, community, and workplace. Those who didn't conform were punished, giving rise to the popular Japanese saying:

> *"the nail that sticks out must be hammered back in".*

The Inspector and Sgt. Lee now suspected that the victim at the Presidio may have belonged to the same group or organization as the dead homeless man. Both were Asians and that certainly helps in narrowing the focus of their investigation. But the central problem remains: who are these dead men with tattooed numbers in their armpits? To get anywhere, it was urgent that they establish a connection between the man buried at the Presidio and the victim at his gravesite.

* * *

Sgt. Lee could scarcely believe his luck the next morning when he arrived for work. At his desk was a thick envelope from the Veterans Office. He nervously fumbled around, looking for a letter opener, as he tried to pry open the brown government envelope. His co-workers noticed the normally calm police veteran acting hurriedly and so much unlike himself.

He flipped through the pages tightly held by a paper fastener and liked what he saw. He grabbed the material, and immediately went to see his partner across the hall right away. He had been worried that the VA would take forever to send them the information they requested. It had happened before, typical of large and understaffed government agencies. As far as he was concerned, the new computer system installed at the relocated VA facility has already paid for itself. The Inspector couldn't be more pleased. Sgt. Lee pointed out that:

"His DD14 Armed Forces separation papers shows that he was a medic during World War II with the famed Japanese-American 442 Combat Regimental team. I'm telling you this guy must have been something else. He was wounded twice in combat and was awarded the Silver Star in Italy."

"The 442nd was the most decorated army unit during the war. But where do we go from here? Again, what was his connection, if any, to the Presidio victim? What did he do before the war? Where did he live",

the Inspector asked?

"His records show a Salinas address."

"Then he had to be one of the thousands of Japanese-Americans

who were sent to internment camps after Pearl Harbor."

"Right, so let's find out if he has any family still living there. Mrs. Chiba might still be in touch with some of them."

"I'll get on it right away",

replied the Sergeant. That said, the Inspector decided to take the rest of the afternoon off. He needed it to clear his head, exhausted from long hours on the job since the Presidio incident. He had also read in the weekend Chronicle that the stripers were biting in Marin County. No one had to nudge him to hurry out the door when the fishing is good.

He soaked in the warm sun at the pier and caught a few *"keepers"* stripers. He enjoyed the fishing at McNears beach in San

Rafael. He gave away the kingfish and skates to the locals who were also fishing that day. On the way back to the city later in the day, he stopped at Margaritaville in Sausalito to indulge in his favorite enchiladas and Corona beer. Life is good he thought as he gazed across the Bay at the San Francisco skyline and fondly remembered his wife. This used to be her favorite watering hole in the Bay Area.

IV - Humble Rise

"Any man who wants to master the essence of my strategy must research diligently, training morning and evening. Thus, can he polish his skill, become free from self and realize extraordinary ability. He will come to possess miraculous power."

Miyamoto Musashi: Book of Five Rings

The rapid rise of Japan as a modern nation began during the Meiji period. The Meiji era (1868-1912) represents one of the most remarkable periods in the history of nations. A modern nation with modern industries, modern political institutions, and a modern pattern of society was created. In the first years of his reign, Emperor Meiji transferred the imperial capital from Kyoto to Edo, the seat of the former feudal government. The city was renamed Tokyo, meaning "eastern capital." A constitution was promulgated, establishing a cabinet and bicameral legislature. The old classes into which society had been divided during the feudal age were abolished. The whole country threw itself with energy and enthusiasm into the study and adoption of modern Western civilization.

But before the nineteenth century ended, the country became involved in the Sino-Japanese

War of 1894-95, which ended in victory for Japan. One consequence of the war was Japan's acquisition of Taiwan from China. Ten years later, in the Russo-Japanese War of 1904-05, Japan once again emerged victorious, acquiring South Sakhalin, which it had ceded to Russia in 1875 in exchange for the Kurile Islands, and having its special interests in Manchuria recognized. After excluding other powers from exercising any influence over Korea, Japan first made Korea its protectorate in 1905 and then annexed it in 1910.

Emperor Meiji, whose enlightened and imaginative rule had helped to guide the nation through the dynamic decades of transformation died in 1912, before the outbreak of World War I. By the end of this war, which Japan entered under the provisions of the Anglo-Japanese Alliance of 1902, Japan was recognized as one of the world's great powers. Emperor Taisho, who succeeded Emperor Meiji, was in turn succeeded by Emperor Hirohito in 1926, and the Showa era began.

* * *

In 1925, Franklin D. Roosevelt was Assistant Secretary of the Navy. His Excellency Takeo Nomura was the Japanese Ambassador to the United States. The State Department was having a reception for visiting foreign dignitaries at the Willard Hotel, several blocks away from the White House. Members of the diplomatic corps including Washington's most powerful and influential citizens were in attendance. Most of the guests milled around the buffet tables. The politically well-connected pulled up chairs so they would be level with Secretary Roosevelt and his wife.

Notable among the foreign dignitaries in attendance was Captain Isoroku Yamamoto, a senior Japanese Navy officer. He accompanied the Japanese Ambassador to the reception. As the senior ranking military officer posted at the Japanese embassy in Washington, the War Department kept a lengthy dossier on him ever since Japan emerged as a world power in the aftermath of the World War 1. Secretary Roosevelt had seen it. Its summary read as follows:

"He was born Takano Isoroku on April 4, 1884, in the small village of Kushigun Sonshomura near Nagaoka, Niigata Prefecture. His father was Sadayoshi Teikichi, a lower-ranking samurai, who gave him the name Isoroku. It meant fifty-six in Japanese, as he was that age when Yamamoto was born.

At 16, Isoroku enrolled in the Imperial Japanese Naval Academy at Etajima, off the shore of Hiroshima. After graduating from the Naval Academy in 1904, Yamamoto served on the Japanese cruiser Nisshin during the Russo-Japanese War. On the Nisshin, during the Battle of Tsushima, which was part of the protective screen for Admiral Togo Heihachiro's flagship Mikasa, Isoroku observed firsthand the tactics of one of the world's greatest admirals. From Togo, he learned, above all things, the need for surprise in battle.

In 1916, Isoroku was adopted by the wealthy and prestigious Yamamoto family and, at a formal ceremony in a Buddhist temple, took the Yamamoto name. Such adoptions were common among Japanese families lacking a male heir, who sought a means of carrying on the family name. It was a common practice for samurai families lacking sons to adopt suitable young men in this fashion to carry on the family name, the rank and the income that comes with it.

He learned to speak fluent English while attending the U.S. Naval War College and Harvard University from 1919-1921. From January, 1926 until March of 1928, Yamamoto served as naval attaché to the Japanese embassy in Washington, a position which was there to investigate America's military might. His tour as an admiral's aide, and two postings as naval attaché in Washington D.C had given him an understanding of the military and material resources available to the Americans.

He traveled extensively in the United States during his two postings there. He also studied American customs and business practices, concentrating on the oil industry. He pointed out that the Imperial Navy and the entire Japanese economy depended on imports of raw materials from the United States.

Physically, the file described Yamamoto as five feet three inches in height and stocky built with broad shoulders. He had full lips, angular jaws which slanted sharply to chin and large well-spaced eyes. His commanding face subdued all of the trappings of his Imperial Navy uniform including the massive epaulets and a thick chest crowded with orders and medals."

Off the record, Yamamoto practiced calligraphy while other military leaders avoided it to dispel the image of being *"soft"* warriors. Yamamoto enjoyed calligraphy very much and was highly skilled with the brush. He was an accomplished man in so many ways in addition to being a military genius.

The history of Japanese calligraphy begins with importing the Chinese writing system, namely Kanji, which in Japanese means *"characters of China"* in the early fifth century. At that time, the Chinese writing system was already fully matured and developed. There were approximately 50,000 kanji in circulation and five major styles in calligraphy. However, since Japanese linguistics and grammar are different from Chinese, it became necessary to create unique calligraphy styles that are exclusively used in Japan, such as Kana. The first real Japanese style, called *"Wayoushodou"*, meaning Japanese style calligraphy was introduced by Ono No Michikaze. Japanese literature and calligraphy subsequently deviated from Chinese aesthetics.

Admiral Yamamoto has an outstanding calligraphy to his credit. The kanji on the work reads *"Shinseichimei"*, meaning "pure emotion and clean intelligence" He signed it with his pen name, *"Choryou"*, which was a literary name of his hometown of Nagaoka.

His relationship with geisha women was also widely known among his circle of friends. Naturally, the geisha houses of his mistresses were decorated with his much-admired calligraphy. He was an avid gambler as well, enjoying shogi, billiards, bridge, mahjong, poker and other games that tested and sharpened his wits. He once remarked:

> *"If I can keep 5,000 ideographs in my mind, it is not hard to keep in mind 52 cards."*

He frequently made jokes about moving to Monaco and starting his own casino. He earned a large second income from his winnings at bridge and poker.

* * *

As the Secretary and Mrs. Roosevelt comingled with the guests, they inadvertently found themselves engaged in polite conversation with the Japanese Ambassador. However, when Mr. Roosevelt casually asked the Ambassador a question about the future role of its navy in the Pacific, the latter quite naturally deferred the question to his senior naval attaché, Captain Isoroku Yamamoto. The unassuming officer confidently replied:

> *"We must ensure the freedom of the seas, Mr. Secretary".*

Roosevelt, of course, knew what Yamamoto really meant. He was merely being discreet in referring to the oil sea lanes from the Middle East. Being an astute student of history himself, it was perhaps no coincidence either that Secretary Roosevelt singled out the Japanese Ambassador in inquiring about the future role of the Imperial Japanese Navy in the Pacific. After all, it wasn't that long ago that the first group of three Japanese ambassadors to the United States stayed at the Willard with seventy-four other delegates in 1860. It was the first time an official Japanese delegation traveled to a foreign destination, and many tourists and journalists gathered to see the sword-carrying Japanese.

The Willard, a historic luxury hotel located two blocks east of the White House in Washington, D.C., was the favored venue for that evening's gala affair. Its initial structures were built in 1816, until they were combined and enlarged into a four-story building and renamed the Willard Hotel after its founder: Henry Willard. The present twelve story structure, designed by famed hotel architect Henry Janeway Hardenbergh, opened in 1901. For many years, the Willard was the only hotel from which one could easily visit all of downtown Washington, and consequently it had housed many dignitaries during its history.

The hotel was also known as *"the residence of presidents"* because every president since Franklin Pierce has either slept in or attended an event there at least once. When the President of the United States was on the premises, it would fly the presidential flag. It has been said that it was the habit of Ulysses S. Grant to drink whiskey and smoke a cigar while relaxing in the lobby. Also, Woodrow Wilson's plans for the League of Nations took shape in the hotel's lobby in 1916. General of the Armies, John J. *"Blackjack"* Pershing, met with hundreds of his officers, many of them combat veterans of World War I, at the Willard Hotel on October 2, 1922.

* * *

Yamamoto's reply pleased the equally well-informed Secretary's wife, Eleanor. And so, ever mindful of who was in attendance among her guests, she didn't waste any time in introducing Captain Yamamoto to another single guest. She was a young American female flyer: Amelia Earhart, a celebrity in her own right.

Yamamoto seemed nervous as he extended his hand to the confident-bearing flyer. For a moment, he had forgotten that he was in a foreign land and instinctively expected the woman to bow low to him as they did in his native Japan. He sensed a strange attraction to the woman flyer. She was not attractive nor was she well-endowed physically. She was thin and had a shapely long neck. The chance meeting made him a little uncomfortable. He had never experienced this sort of attraction before.

To be sure, as a young man, Yamamoto had found the local girls in school attractive, but that was different then. Now, he was already married. Furthermore, the woman was not like him, that is to say, not Asian, he thought to himself. The introduction was brief with the usual mutual exchange of pleasures in meeting and the friendly smiles. But the young female flyer's eyes revealed more. She said that she has always been fascinated by the East and that someday she would very much like to visit Japan.

Secretary Roosevelt, the consummate politician, was oblivious to all of this as his wife was introducing the next group of

Washington luminaries to him. Having had their turn, the Captain and his new acquaintance proceeded to helping themselves to small plates of local delicacies: crab cakes from the Chesapeake and shrimp from Norfolk. Then they drifted out on the veranda to enjoy the cool evening air and further engage in polite conversation:

"For someone in your position, you must get to attend a lot of these kinds of functions in Washington, Captain."

"Regretfully, yes. It's part of my job", as he smiled.

"I take that to mean that some have been better than others."

"You are correct! However, I must confess that the food has always been very good as you can see for yourself."

Yamamoto was staring at his slightly pudgy waistline at the same time. Spontaneous laughter erupted between them, unaware that some of the guests' prying eyes had been set in motion. It's been rumored in Washington diplomatic circles that Yamamoto had a keen eye for the ladies despite being a married man. They had barely finished eating the portions on their plates when Ambassador Nomura signaled that it was time to leave.

The short drive back to the Japanese Ambassador's residence on Massachusetts' Avenue seemed to take longer than usual that evening. And for some unexplained reason, Yamamoto's memories of his youth suddenly overcame him. The acquaintance he had made earlier that evening with the youthful American flyer must have brought on this, he said to himself. His thoughts were also of his father and his birthplace of Nagaoka in 1884.

* * *

Morning couldn't come soon enough and Yamamoto was in good spirits. It was a beautiful autumn day in Washington and oak leaves were changing color and fluttering to the ground in the light breeze. Winter was still a couple of months away and city residents were glad to see the hot and humid summer gone. He was thinking of the young lady he met just a few short hours ago. He wanted to see her again, discreetly of course. He was aware of the differences in their cultures, not to mention the societal taboos of the time. It was all right to be seen together in public in Washington D.C. but across the Potomac in Virginia, one had to be more careful, since racial fraternization was not accepted in polite American society in those days. In fact, interracial marriages were illegal in most of the South. This was not surprising to Yamamoto since similar notions and mores existed in

Japan based on class instead of a person's skin color. Still, no self-respecting Japanese women of his time were permitted to become romantically involved with a *"gaijin"* or barbarian, as it were.

The past always seems to come back to him whenever his emotions were stirred. He wondered why it happened to him all the time. Whenever he was faced with this kind of a problem, he sought refuge in the knowledge that others who came before him must have experienced similar circumstances. He told himself that by learning from someone else's mistakes, he can become a better person and consequently lead a more meaningful life. Who can argue with that logic, he asked himself? When he was a young man, he remembered reading Aristotle, the Greek philosopher, who said that:

"Too much of anything in life is not good."

Then, there is also the so-called *"Golden Rule"* which basically says:

"Do not do to others what you don't want them to do to you."

But what do these lifelong guiding principles he has lived by all of his life, have to with his desire to further his acquaintance with Amelia Earhart anyway? Why was he experiencing all of these mixed-up emotions so early in the day he thought? It was out of character for him to be thinking about all of these things. Rationalizing to himself, he was already a middle-aged adult male after all.

Life had been hard for Yamamoto's family in his youth. Japan was a nation in transition from a feudal economy. In school, his family could not afford textbooks so he took it upon himself to meticulously copy the text by hand. This diligence was to serve him well later in life. During those formative years, he also learned about the West and Christianity from American missionaries. Although he never became a Christian himself, he kept a Bible on his bookshelf throughout his life. This early exposure gave him the rare ability to look at Japan's situation from an international viewpoint, and he was able to develop the ability to make dispassionate and logical observations.

Yamamoto was content to spend the rest of the day reminiscing about the past and thinking about Miss Earhart, when a member of the embassy household staff interrupted him with a note. He thought nothing of it, as messages were routine for a man of his position and so he quickly dismissed the messenger. However, across the Potomac in a private residence for single women, Amelia wondered if her note had arrived. She didn't consider her action unconventional although many of her contemporaries might have disagreed. It was not in her nature to worry about what others thought about her. She had been a nonconformist since her childhood. Alone in her room reading, intermittent thoughts about her childhood also kept her restless.

Born in Atchison, Kansas during its heyday on July 24, 1897 in her grandparents' home, her father was an attorney and her mother a homemaker. Historical records document the Lewis and Clark expedition having camped on the hills here on their way west. Several decades later, it served as a hub along the Atchison, Topeka & Santa Fe Railway.

From the earliest days of her childhood, Amelia demonstrated an attitude of daring and confidence. When she was seven, her father took the family to St. Louis for the World's fair. She was so impressed by the roller coaster that she decided to build her own with her sister and friends. They attached the track to the roof of a shed and greased it with lard. She was the first to ride the new *"thriller"*. She zoomed down the track and crashed. Still, she jumped up from the wreckage and shouted, *"It's just like flying"*. The same adventurous girl would later in life become more than just a record-setting pilot, but also a social worker, writer, and a feminist, decades ahead of her time.

She grew up in Kansas City in a home her grandfather gave her mother and father as a wedding gift. The years spent there were happy for her and Pidge, a younger sister, who both enjoyed *"tomboyish activities"*. The usual skirts and pinafores of the time were completely unsuited to their play, so their mother hired a woman to make gym suits, pleated bloomers that came down to their knees. While the girls spent a great deal of time with their grandparents, they enjoyed the companionship of their father the most. He read stories to them and even made up his own wild tales of adventure.

While still brooding about the previous night's meeting with Yamamoto, she was abruptly interrupted by one of the other boarders calling her to the phone. She had hoped it would be Yamamoto and so she ran downstairs and dashed across the hallway to the guest parlor to get to the phone. It was Yoshi, the same elderly member of the embassy staff who had handed her note to Yamamoto. In a distinctly foreign accent, the elderly man politely asked her if she could meet the Captain at noon later that day at the Smithsonian. She readily consented, her face gleaming with flirtatious joy.

* * *

Yamamoto wore his best Sunday suit. He always liked wearing finely tailored Western style suits, a nice change from the naval uniform he had to wear to work and at embassy functions. He was looking forward to seeing the young lady flyer again, but he was trying to decide where to take her after the meeting at the Smithsonian. He felt that they would be too conspicuous at the grounds on the mall, a favorite weekend outing for Washingtonians. He knew that there would be a large crowd there and that he might be recognized by someone from the diplomatic community. He thought that the Washington Navy Yard might be a better choice, since entry there is restricted to the general public.

Amelia was punctual, arriving in a cab from Arlington, Virginia just a short ride across the Potomac. She was wearing a pale blue suit and flat shoes, out of deference to Yamamoto's shorter stature. They smiled at each other as he motioned her across the mall to the Art Gallery.

"I hope I haven't kept you waiting long", she remarked.

"Not at all; I purposely came early to make sure that you weren't kept waiting. I'm often reminded by my peers that punctuality is an admirable trait,"

he replied.

"I couldn't agree more." It's a beautiful day too, isn't it?

"Yes indeed. Would you like to take a little walk first and enjoy the autumn air?"

Exchanging additional remarks about the beautiful weather, they strolled under the tall trees. Suddenly, Yamamoto stopped and turned to Amelia. He grabbed her elbow and steered her back towards the Smithsonian.

"I saw someone I recognized from the Embassy. Perhaps, it would be a good idea if we went elsewhere. Is that all right with you?"

"I understand. Why don't we get a taxi and go someplace less crowded?"

No sooner had she suggested taking a cab, one conveniently pulled up next to the curb. Yamamoto asked the driver to take them to the Navy Yard in Southeast Washington. No one would be there on a Sunday afternoon and the guard at the main gate would give only a cursory glance to a high ranking foreign naval officer's ID card.

V - Pacific Destiny

"The love of flying is the love of beauty. It was more beautiful up there than anything I had known,"

Amelia Earhart

The elder of two daughters of an alcoholic railroad lawyer and a genteel mother, Earhart seemed to have been born with a daredevil streak. Her mother catered to it, dressing her in bloomers, outfits that "shocked all the nice little girls" as Amelia later put it, in their town of Atchison, Kansas. With bloomers billowing, she'd speed downhill on her sled, belly down, the way boys did it. She popped off rats with a .22 in her grandfather's barn and explored the dark caves in the cliffs above the Missouri River. To Earhart, learning to fly seemed no more daring than these stunts, and by 1921 she had a license to compete.

Seven years later, while working with the immigrant children in Boston, she received a phone call from Capt. Hilton H. Railey, a former Army pilot. Would she, Railey asked, be willing to fly across the Atlantic? Amelia said: "Yes, who would refuse such a shining adventure?"

Railey had been chartered by George Putnam, the publisher and public relations whiz who later married Earhart, to find a woman pilot capable of flying the Atlantic. Putnam had made a best-seller out of Lindbergh's post-flight account. He now wanted to manage a similar flight by a woman. Amelia's name was the first to pop up; she spent her weekends flying at an airport near Boston and had been noticed by one of Railey's friends who thought her "earnest." Her resemblance to Lindbergh, then the most famous man in the world, clinched the deal.

* * *

The Museum at the Navy Yard in Southeast Washington D.C. had never been a popular hangout for tourists on late autumn

Sunday afternoons. The cold wind blowing from the Potomac, signaling the approach of a freezing winter didn't help make that particular day any more pleasant. Slate grey clouds seemed to have come from nowhere. Even the usually plentiful seagulls that fed on migrating Chesapeake perch suddenly vanished, instinctively obeying Mother Nature's call to seek warmer waters elsewhere. A few sailors could be seen on their way to the mess hall, were so busy talking about their assignments the following work day, shoulders hunched against the intermittent gale.

Yamamoto and Amelia got out of the cab in front of the Navy Yard Museum which was just inside the compound. No one noticed the foreign visitor and his lady companion making a dash to the side entrance of the modest brick building. To their good fortune, they managed to quietly sneak inside without being noticed by a frail-looking security guard posted at the visitor's entrance.

Yamamoto told Amelia that there is a portrait in the main hall of a delegation of Japanese samurai who visited the Yard during the 1860s. He thought that she might find it interesting. And right he was! Amelia was impressed with the somewhat faded group portrait of over fifty men decked in their samurai regalia and swords.

> *"Most of them must be quite old now or passed away. Did you know any of them"*, she asked?

> *"No, I'm sorry to say. Do I look that ancient to you?"*

Yamamoto replied grinning at the same time. He appeared to be puzzled by her question although he elicited a high-pitched laughter from her. Perhaps, she was just being herself, funny and carefree, he thought. Meanwhile, Amelia was drawn ever closer to the individual faces in the portrait, and then turned to face him:

"I don't know anything about you, Captain. Would you mind telling me a bit about your career in the Navy?"

"I thought I just did",

as he bowed to show his respect to his fellow warriors in the portrait.

"Really, I can't read your mind; you know that! What did you really mean the other night at the Willard hotel, when you replied to President Roosevelt that you wanted to ensure the freedom of the seas?"

"I was merely trying to point out that all countries should observe absolute freedom of navigation upon the seas, outside their territorial waters. It's nothing new where international law is concerned, stressing freedom to navigate the oceans. It was one of the Fourteen Points proposed by President Woodrow Wilson at the Peace Conference in Paris in the aftermath of World War I."

"I'm somewhat familiar with its basic concepts and as you said, it's a principle law of the sea that has been observed by numerous countries for a long time. It's also referred to as 'mare liberum' which means free sea in Latin",

added the young flyer. You're correct!

"It goes back more than three hundred years ago. In 1609, Dutch jurist and philosopher Hugo Grotius wrote what is considered the foundation of the international legal doctrine regarding the seas and oceans. While it is generally assumed that Grotius first propounded the principle of freedom of the seas, countries in the Indian Ocean and other Asian seas accepted the right of unobstructed navigation long before Grotius wrote his De Jure Praedae (On the Law of Spoils) in 1604.

Previously, in the 16th century, Spanish theologian Francisco de Vitoria postulated the idea of freedom of the seas in a more rudimentary fashion under the principles of jus gentium."

Yamamoto abruptly stopped talking and brought his right hand, palm up, to wipe his face.

"Please accept my apologies, Miss Earhart. I started to lecture, as though you were one of my junior officers attending class aboard ship. I must be boring you now."

"No, not at all. It's a fascinating and complex subject - freedom of the seas. I'm sure, there is so much more that you can tell me",

said the young lady aviator. The couple simultaneously nodded in agreement, leaving no doubt at how much they also seemed to enjoy each other's company. Both looked at their watches and realized that it was getting late in the day. But they were alone and didn't care. They were happy together, but not wishing to put the Captain in an awkward position, Amelia quickly revived their conversation in almost a whispering tone, sensing the mutual desire for discretion:

"Remember the other night at the reception? I mentioned then that I wanted to learn so much about Japan. The books and magazine articles I've read about your country never seemed to tell a complete story. Perhaps, it's because they were all written by Westerners who never lived there at all, much less spoke and read Japanese.

Their impressions of Japan could have only been experienced through the eyes of a foreigner, who might have visited the country once or twice in their entire life. Do you understand what I'm trying to say? For instance, what do you consider unique about Japan", she asked?

Yamamoto was caught off-guard by the sincerity of Amelia's curiosity, not expecting the academic nature of her question. Most American and European women he had met in the past would have engaged him instead in casual conversation about Japanese cuisine or etiquette. Fumbling for words, but at the same time challenged, Yamamoto could only say:

"Please, give me a moment to think."

"That may take all day,"

she responded, laughing at the same time while trying to cover her mouth with her hands, something any Japanese male would have noticed a bit odd for an American woman to do.

Yamamoto was reminded of how Japanese women often covered their mouths with their hands when they laughed. But, in most instances, they used their ornately decorated fans instead, further adding to their femininity. He couldn't help smiling either, as he had been utterly taken by the young woman's wit and sense of humor.

"There is so much to tell that I don't know where exactly to begin. So, let's limit our discussion to those things which are obvious even to the Japanese."

"Like what", her eyebrows slightly lifted?

"Chotto, I'm sorry, I meant, I'm getting there", as he raised his head to acquiesce his companion.

"The Japanese revere the cherry tree. Let me tell you its beautiful story.

The cherry is called in the Japanese language 'sakura,' named for Princess Kono-hana-sakuya-Hime, who is enshrined on the top of Mt. Fuji. This long name means "tree-flowers-blooming-princess," because, it is said, she dropped from heaven upon a cherry tree. Hence, the cherry blossom is considered to be the national flower of Japan.

The cherry is extensively cultivated in Japan, though it grows wild on plains and in deep mountains in the country. In one respect, it symbolizes the national character of the Japanese, as in the life of a samurai during our feudal era.

The samurai was compared to the short-lived cherry-blossoms, which lasted no more than three days, for he was always fully prepared to sacrifice his life at any time in the service of his master. And so, what the cherry is among flowers is what the samurai is among men."

Amelia was so entranced by the story that she unknowingly drew herself physically close to Yamamoto and that their hands momentarily touched. She never expected to hear it told so expressively from, least of all, a Japanese warrior such as Yamamoto. Her admiration of his intellect and genuine emotions grew as she absorbed every delicate word uttered in a deep foreign tone. She pleaded to tell her more about the Japanese cherry tree.

"The Japanese are proud of their sakura, because no other people have it. The sakura is quite different from the cherry of other countries. To differentiate it from the fruit bearing varieties seen in

many countries, the Japanese sakura are called the Japanese flowering cherry in English.

Poets and artists have always been eager to depict the loveliness of the blossom in words and colors. Sakura is called the flower of flowers, and when the Japanese use the word 'hana' or flower, it means sakura. Hanami or flower viewing means the viewing of sakura blossoms and no other flowers.

The blooming period of sakura is very short, and in a few days the flower is scattered away in the spring breeze. So, the people are long accustomed to stop their daily work or close up their shops to have sakura viewing picnics at the best and convenient places. It is the merriest occasion of the year, with drinks, music and song.

On the other hand, some persons prefer to enjoy the blossom quietly and leisurely, and select remote mountain or seashore regions which are not frequented by many people."

"Someday, I would like to see the sakura trees of Japan; that probably won't ever happen though",

she said, with a somber look on her face. She stumbled slightly on a step when they were making another turn in the maze of naval exhibits and he grabbed her arm to keep her from falling.

"I'm so clumsy. It's amazing how I can fly when I can hardly walk straight sometimes."

He kept his arm under hers; they continued their tour of the museum. He looked rather flushed and would not look at her directly. Amelia whispered quietly*:*

"I may not get to Japan to see the cherry blossoms anytime soon, but I think a warm cup of coffee is something we can arrange to have on the premises."

"Yes, that is a good idea; but, surely a cup of hot sake would taste better on this cold day",

replied Yamamoto. Amelia looked a bit surprised:

"I've heard of sake, but where on earth can you get that here in the Yard; at your embassy, perhaps?"

That was all Yamamoto needed to hear.

"Have you forgotten who you're with?"

Embarrassed and covering her mouth again, Amelia could only say:

"I think that would be a cultural first for me."

He turned to her again, his brown eyes lively and expressive:

"What is that American expression? There is a first time for everything, you know!"

In leaving the museum, they headed toward the main gate. The sun shone briefly sending shafts of light over the grayish-colored water and then the rain started again. The wind had died down. He raised a large black umbrella for both of them and resumed his hold on her arm. Less than a block outside of the gate, they managed to flag down a passing cab.

* * *

When they arrived at the Japanese Embassy compound, Yamamoto directed the cab driver to enter a side entrance normally used only by the staff. They both understood the need for discretion, wary of being seen together in public, had they entered inside the visitor's entrance at 2520 Massachusetts Avenue. Yamamoto pointed out that it was erected in 1931, in the Georgian Revival architectural style, with subtle elements of Japanese architecture, and that Emperor Hirohito allegedly approved the design personally.

In addition to serving as Japan's diplomatic mission in the United States, the embassy also provided Japanese consular services to residents of the District of Columbia, Virginia, and Maryland. Its original design consisted of the ambassador's residence, two Chancery buildings with strong Japanese architectural influence, a tea house, a tennis court, a gym, and other recreational facilities. The embassy featured a cobblestone courtyard and driveway in front of the building. The grounds were landscaped to complement Rock Creek Park, which abuts the rear of the embassy grounds.

The couple was met by Yoshi, one of the longest serving elderly attendants at the embassy. He bowed to the pair and quickly offered to help them with their coats. He then inquired:

"Would the Captain and the lady like some refreshments, perhaps?"

Yamamoto enthusiastically answered back:

"Hai, bring us the finest bottle of sake from the cellar; the Yoshinogawa brand from Niigata Prefecture."

Redirecting his attention to his American female guest, he added:

"You know Japanese sake was first distilled from rice around 2,000 years ago, but it was not until the Edo period, lasting from 1615 and 1867, that the present-day clear sake was made. Sake, depending on the brand and quality, ranges from 32 to 40 proof.

Yoshinogawa is the oldest sake brewery in Japan. It was established in 1548 in Niigata prefecture which has a reputation for producing some of the best Japanese sake. The primary reason for this is that Niigata grows some of the best rice in the world. The taste and quality of sake is said to hinge greatly on the water used."

"And why is that",

asked Amelia?

"Well, in the case of the Yoshinogawa Brewery in Niigata, my hometown, the sake there is brewed with specific and delicate water, 'Tenka Kanrosen', which translates to 'Sweet Water of Heaven and Earth'. It is water that comes from a spring and combined with that from Japan's largest river, the Shinano River, plus melted snow from Nigata's eastern mountain range. It is a soft water, yet rich in minerals that promote yeast growth.

Since 1548, Yoshinogawa has been using this water to brew its clean and smooth lasting sake. Much is therefore owed to the Shinano-gawa River leading into exceptionally fertile rice cultivation. If I sound biased, it's perhaps because Niigata is my ancestral home.

Make no mistake; however, there are also other brewery production centers in Japan such as Kyoto, Aomori, and Hyogo, where one can experience exclusive styles and flavors of sake. Nada, near Kobe, is noted for its "miyamizu" (shrine water) and it still is one of the great sake brewery centers of Japan."

Of course, I understand. But when was sake first made and how it is produced?

"Alcoholic beverages are mentioned several times in the Kojiki, Japan's first written history, which was compiled in 712. The probable origin of true sake was during the Nara period (710 -794). There

are two basic types: Futsū-shu, or ordinary sake and Tokutei meishō-shu or special-designation sake. The former is the equivalent of table wine and accounts for the majority of sake produced. Tokutei meishō-shu refers to premium sakes differentiated by the degree to which the rice has been polished and the added percentage of brewer's alcohol or the absence of such additives."

"Are there different types or grades like in whisky or scotch? And are some more expensive than others?"

"Yes, there are three grades of sake: Tokkyu (special deluxe), Ikkyu (first class), and Nikyu (second class) and prices differ accordingly. In general, however, sake is judged by the harmonious blend of the so-called five tastes: sweetness, sourness, acridity,

astringency, and bitterness. The brands of sake are commonly classified as ama-kuchi (sweet types) and kara-kuchi (acrid types).

Traditional methods of brewing have been replaced by the most modern and scientific techniques, but the spirit of sake production still remains the same."

"How fascinating! You obviously have taken a lot of time to learn about sake. I've learned so much about Japan from you in the short time we've known each other",

the young aviatrix responded, clearly impressed by her host.

"I have so much more to tell you, but I sound like I'm lecturing to you again. You

must be famished by now from all of the day's activities. And, I talk too much,"

sounding almost apologetically. The Captain then summoned Yoshi one more time:

"Do we have any more of those scrumptious pastries the French Ambassador brought by yesterday? Bring us some, please! We'll be in the morning room."

"Don't feel rushed. I still have all afternoon and most of the evening before I'm expected back at my residence",

Amelia hastened to add.

"That's wonderful. Let's take the elevator. The morning room is on the second floor."

The elevator rose slowly, squeaking intermittently. The inside was paneled with dark wood that had been lacquered and was inset at intervals with small rectangular mirrors that reflected their figures in the dim ceiling light. When they got out, Yamamoto directed Amelia to the second door on the left. The halls were covered in striped paper that was cream and black. Amelia could hear typing nearby. All of the other doors had a nameplate on them with some kind of writing in Japanese. Amelia had no idea what went on behind the doors.

Because it was by this time early afternoon, the room was not as brightly lit as it was most mornings. The east facing windows didn't make a difference on a cloudy day, either. The walls were papered in pale ocher silk with small lotus flowers and cranes in a mixed pattern. Two large windows with darker, almost orange draperies were open to reveal the cloudy day and the garden below. An old

Federalist style fireplace with painted white brick took up most of one wall. Two comfortable sofas in an olive-green color flanked the fireplace. Between them was a long oval table with several magazines and books with English titles.

End tables held silver-based lamps with elaborate scrolled edges. Several water colors were in white frames on two walls. The pictures were all seascapes; no boats. Amelia noticed only waves and beach. Book cases were on either side of the door and a tall secretary desk in dark wood was open to reveal writing paper and pens. The wood looked similar to the elevator's elegant black lacquer. Except for the wallpaper, the room didn't look particularly oriental. It reminded Amelia of pictures of rooms in old colonial Virginia homes. One of the windows had a cushioned gold brocade covered window seat. Amelia sat on this first.

"This is a lovely room and what a beautiful view. You must have a professional gardener on the embassy staff",

she commented.

Yamamoto walked over and gazed out at the walled garden with the small trees and a fish pond.

"Yes, he would be my secretary's younger brother and he is quite talented. It is hard to grow some things though in the humid summers. I walk in the garden most evenings and sit on the small bench. I like this room. I read the daily newspapers and other business papers here, in the morning, because it is well lit. In the evenings, I usually read here too for a while and write letters to my family at

the desk. You can't hear the traffic from here and it's restful,"

Just then, Yoshi entered the room with a bottle of fine sake from the Yoshinogawa brewery and said that he'd be back soon with the French pastries. Amelia fortuitously switched the topic of conversation. She was adept at doing that, skillfully manipulating conversations to her liking at a moment's notice without anyone seemingly offended by it.

"Is the story of sake as wonderful as that of the sakura?

Yamamoto replied:

"Perhaps the story about sake is better told as we're emptying the bottle".

"You mean to tell me that we're going to drink the entire bottle? I must warn you, Sir. I may not leave much for you."

Yamamoto burst into laughter.

"Don't worry; there is a cellar full of it. First, I'll fill your cup and then mine. Afterwards, you fill my cup and then yours, until the sake bottle is empty."

The sake cups were small and white and decorated with a black crane flying across the surface. Amelia commented on their small size.

"It may take a while to drink the whole bottle."

As Yoshi took leave, Yamamoto poured her the first cup, commenting at the same time, that the cups must never be left empty afterwards because that would be considered rude in Japan.

"Kempai", exclaimed Yamamoto!

"It's the same as saying 'cheers' or 'bottoms up'."

Amelia closed her eyes as she gulped her first tiny cup and then opened them wide and smiled, remarking:

"Wow, superb!"

Yamamoto was pleased that her guest seemed to like the rice wine. She should, for it was the one of the finest available, reserved for only the wealthy and powerful of Japanese society. Amelia was already beginning to feel the effect of the potent cup of sake. She liked it so much that she decided to help herself to more. As she reached for the bottle, she felt the hand of her host on hers saying:

"No, no; remember what I said earlier that the host has to pour the sake for his guest. After that, the guest reciprocates by filling the cup of the host. It is the etiquette. It is your first time to experience this and you should not be embarrassed."

"But I am in a way, because I always like to do things right the first time; I don't like to make mistakes",

replied Amelia.

"I understand perfectly what you are saying; I am like you. That is why I drink my sake slowly or else I get drunk quickly."

Both individuals laughed out loud. Yamamoto had succeeded in diplomatically advising his guest to sip her cup of sake instead of downing it in one gulf like a shot of whiskey.

A moment later, a discreet knock was heard. It was Yoshi again, but this time he rolled a serving cart into the room. The food was artistically arranged on celadon dishes: perfectly browned Japanese dumplings or gyoza, shrimp cocktail, a clear broth with seaweed, thinly sliced shitake mushrooms, and off to one side were French pastries. Amelia exclaimed:

"It all looks so delicious. It's much more than the cup of coffee that you had suggested we have earlier today."

"It's nothing really; it's Japanese hospitality, offering the best for our

honored guest. Besides, it is our first dinner together and I wanted to make a first good impression. I'm sorry that we could not have it in a more elegant restaurant in the city."

Amelia then asked her host:

"What are these dumplings called? They resemble Polish pirogues my grandmother made when I was growing up in Kansas."

"Those dumplings are called gyoza; they are very popular in Japan. The filling can be pork, shrimp or vegetable",

replied Yamamoto.

"It looks great; what a marvelous tray Yoshi created!"

They were enjoying their dinner, finishing off with the dainty French pastries until they were yet interrupted by Yoshi again. He asked if the couple needed anything else. Perhaps, they wanted more refreshments such as coffee or tea after dinner. Yamamoto declined with a simple bow, a signal to Yoshi that everything was fine and that he should retire for the day. But as Yoshi was about to leave the room, Amelia asked him where she could refresh herself a bit after dinner. She was shown the powder room in the hallway.

Amelia noticed that the sake cups were once more filled when she returned. But there was something else. The lights were dimmed and music was playing in the background. It sounded like Foxtrot from the beat. Yamamoto extended his hand in invitation and Amelia gladly accepted. She was a little rusty but Yamamoto helped her gain her rhythm in no time at all. He told her that he gets a lot of practice dancing at all of the embassy receptions he attends in Washington's diplomatic circle. Agreeing with him, she then proceeded to take off her heels, so that they would be more comfortable, embraced at the same height, more or less.

Yamamoto was about to give her a short course on how to stay in place while dancing when Amelia deftly raised her left hand and gently placed it over his mouth. At the same time, she covered her own and gestured him to keep quiet as she moved closer to him in a deeper embrace. To the experienced senior naval officer, it was clear that the young American flyer had conveyed her attraction to him.

Grinning like an innocent school boy, Yamamoto knew very well what was expected of him for the remainder of that eventful day.

For her part, Amelia made up her mind not to return to her residence across the Potomac that evening.

VI - Eventful Years

"Some Issei like Yuwakichi Sakauye were able to purchase small farmsteads in the early 1900's, before the California Alien Land Laws were enacted...."

Collection of Eichii Edward Sakauye, California History Center Archives

Japanese immigration to the United States, both in Hawaii and the mainland, was primarily driven by the demand for labor. In the 1860s through the 1880s, Japanese laborers were brought in to work in the large sugar plantations in Hawaii. But finding the conditions on the plantations under the contract labor system brutal, many of them sought ways to escape and some eventually made their way to the mainland.

During the same period, California's anti-Chinese movement resulted in the passage of the Chinese Exclusion Act of 1882, which dramatically diminished the numbers of Chinese laborers in the late 1880s and 1890s. As a result, a few Japanese immigrants began to work as agricultural workers filling the vacuum created by the Chinese Exclusion Act. After a short period, a number of Japanese laborers moved out of migrant labor to become independent farmers in their own right. They could become sharecroppers and make contracts with landowners to work the land and split the proceeds of the sale of the crops. If they had some capital, they could also lease or purchase land.

Families were established through the picture bride system and children were born in the United States. Farming communities of settled Japanese families were formed throughout California. Japanese immigrants played an important part in the development of agriculture in the Salinas area.

In 1908 the Salinas Valley Japanese Agricultural Contractors' Association was formed. It was one of the earliest Japanese agricultural cooperative groups in California. Consequently, major political parties both at the local and state levels with the support of organized labor began to protest Japanese immigration and land ownership. And so, in 1913, the California State legislature passed the Alien Land Act prohibiting Aliens ineligible for citizenship from purchasing land and other property. This act was specifically aimed at Japanese farmers, since Asians were ineligible for citizenship and the Japanese were the only group of Asians purchasing land at the time.

By 1920, when the Alien Land Laws forbade Issei or first-generation Japanese immigrants from owning land, they turned to truck farming. Japanese farmers were producing the majority of the tomato and spinach crops. Other important crops included strawberries and later, deciduous fruit trees. By using crops that could be grown and distributed quickly, the Japanese farmers could get around the state laws.

* * *

Ryosako Chiba never wanted to leave home in 1924. He loved the hilly land, the green rice fields and pointy-topped houses. Even as a child, he had nursed sick wild birds and saved the life of the village's dog that had broken a leg in a fall. He dreamed of someday becoming a doctor and to take the place of the elderly doctor in his village. The doctor who cared for them in the town was getting old, past sixty and wanted to retire.

Ryosako's father had sent for medical books and other literature from Osaka for his oldest son to study when he finished high school, because there was not enough family money to pay for medical school. But, his Uncle Jiro in Salinas, California had convinced his mother to let him go and seek a better life in America on their small family farm. He had also heard rumors within the Japanese-American community that President Coolidge was about to sign into law an act that excluded

Japanese immigration. In the end, the entire matter was soon overtaken by political and economic unrest throughout Japan.

After two centuries, the Japanese policy of seclusion under the shoguns of the Edo period came to an end, when the country was opened to trade by American intervention in 1854. The years following the Meiji restoration of 1868 and the fall of the Shogunate had seen Japan transform itself from a feudal society into a modern industrial state.

The Japanese sent delegations and students around the world to learn and assimilate Western arts and sciences with an intention of making Japan equal to the Western powers. But there were also significant internal ramifications felt throughout Japan. The leaders of the Meiji revolution soon turned over their possessions to the Emperor. By 1871, the feudal provinces were made prefectures, their lords became governors, and all the lines of power ran to the Emperor. It was mainly the fact that the Emperor's sacred status was guaranteed by the prefectural leaders that enabled political change.

It was this restoration, and an immediate bid for military power based on the Western nations' examples, that saved Japan from coming under the rule of imperialist forces as did China. British officers took to building the Empire a navy that would be capable of preventing foreign incursions. French army officers restructured the old samurai armies and molded them into an effective fighting force. Dutch engineers took to building necessary infrastructure that could support both the warships bought in Europe and the Armies build up at home. Additional European ideas and ideals came to the modernizing Empire.

A justice system was based on the French model. A system of education was based on the

American model. A system of political liberty was also established based in the still absolute, though nominally, constitutional monarchies in Europe. However, freedom of expression and thought were not among those granted to the Japanese. Furthermore, the American educational model did not prevent the Japanese from introducing even the youngest children to the idea of supreme rule by the Emperor, without argument. Books favorable to democracy were banned, and parties with desires to adopt democracy were forced to abandon their wishes or be banned as well.

And so, a different fate now awaited young Ryosako. His family encouraged him to leave the country for a safer life in America. During that period, the Japanese military had been declining in prestige. No longer were bright students aspiring to join the army or navy. Military officers were wearing civilian clothes when off duty. Thus, in 1926, Japan passed the

Peace Preservation Law which set up military training at universities and high schools.

In Japan's culture wars, peer pressure, economic hardship and incessant government propaganda combined, proved too much to resist even for those who disagreed with the government. Young Japanese males were strongly encouraged to join the Army and fight in China. When Japan waged a protracted war with its giant neighbor, China, the country's national leaders had deliberately decided to pursue a more militaristic foreign policy and began eliminating moderate opposition leaders. The Communist, Socialist and anarchist movements in Japan were decimated, and their publications ceased to exist.

* * *

Ryosako loved his country and would have never agreed to his family wishes if he thought that the war with China was a just cause. But in the end, he had made up his mind to leave and join his mother's older brother, Uncle Jiro, in California. His uncle had made a similar journey to America in 1895, during the first Sino-Japanese war which was fought between the Qing Empire of China and Japan, primarily over influence of Korea. At that time, Korea continued to exclude foreigners, refusing embassies from foreign countries and firing on ships near its shores.

At the start of the war, Japan had the benefit of three decades of reform, leaving Korea outdated and vulnerable. The war demonstrated the failure of the Qing Empire’s attempt to modernize its military and fend off threats to its sovereignty, especially when compared to Japan’s successful Meiji restoration. For the first time, regional dominance in East Asia shifted from China to Japan.

The Meiji government specifically turned to Korea, in order to further their security and national interests. Korea was occupied and declared a Japanese protectorate following the Japan-Korea Treaty of 1905. The Korean Peninsula was officially part of the Empire of Japan for 35 years. During the same period, thousands of Koreans had come to Japan in search of jobs. But, social contacts between Koreans and Japanese were limited. Many Japanese despised the Koreans, disliking the smell of their food and believing them to be inclined toward crime and other unwholesome habits. They thought of Koreans as belonging to an inferior race, and intermarriage between Koreans and Japanese was unthinkable.

In addition to Korea, Japan had earlier occupied the Ryukyu chain in 1878, with Okinawa as the new prefecture capital. Before that, in 1875, the Kuriles Islands to the north had been occupied to provide a buffer against Russian aggression. The ensuing Russo-Japanese War of 1904 to 1905 was a conflict for control of Korea and parts of Manchuria between the Russian Empire and Japan. The war was significant as it was the first modern war in which an Asian country defeated a European power. The victory greatly raised Japan's stature in the world of global politics. Russia's defeat cleared the way for Japan to annex Korea outright in 1910.

Japan entered World War I in 1914, seizing the opportunity of Germany's distraction with the European War, when it sought to expand its sphere of influence in China and the Pacific. Japan declared war on Germany on August 23, 1914. Japanese and allied British Empire forces soon moved to occupy Tsingtao fortress, the German East Asia Squadron base, German-leased territories in China's Shandong Province as well as the Marianas, Caroline, and Marshall

Islands in the Pacific. The siege of Tsingtao proved successful. The German colonial troops surrendered on November 7, 1915. Japan then gained the German holdings.

When World War I began in 1914, Japan was the primary power in the Far East. It possessed the whole of Korea and Formosa, the Ryukyu's, the Bonins, and was able to exercise its power anywhere its fleet would go. Patriotic societies were growing. One of these was the Doka Kai Society which had been founded by university professors.

Like Europe's emerging fascists, the patriotic societies opposed class struggle in favor of national unity. Some of them opposed the existence of parliament. Some opposed what they saw as the corrupting influence caused by money and industrial wealth. Most of them supported their nation's traditional religion and the belief that the Emperor was godly and sacrosanct. They called themselves *"chivalrous patriots."* And some of them were willing to use physical intimidation against scholars, politicians or financiers who were friendly toward democracy. And there were those willing to use violence to intimidate anyone they saw as willing to weaken the Constitution or disseminate *"dangerous thoughts."*

* * *

Call it circumstance or fate, but Ryosako had subconsciously been preparing for this journey years earlier, as he later realized. When he was still in high school, he studied English under the local schoolmaster who had learned English in America during several extended visits with a sister in San Diego. His teacher repeatedly emphasized to him the subtle differences between Japanese and Western culture and often reminded him:

"Do not bow; shake the right hand. Look at them in the eye; otherwise, they think you are dishonest."

Ryosako's traditional Japanese wardrobe was not suitable even for the urban cities in Japan. Western influences had already had an effect on the fashions, another major change brought about during the Meiji era. His parents and other family members managed to pool enough money to buy him a charcoal gray wool coat, a matching hat, a new pair of black shoes plus underwear, extra socks, three shirts, two pairs of pants and a wool jacket. All of the extras were place carefully in a suitcase that had belonged to his late grandfather. His auntie also brought him an umbrella but his father kept that gift because he had read that it rains only during the winter in California. Ryosako's father gave him a homemade money belt with the advice never to take it off.

It was a dreary and foggy morning when he left his village. Smoke straggled up from the rock chimneys. Ryosako's mother packed him some rice cakes to last the two-day trip on foot from his village of Maesawa to Morioka in central Honshu. From there, he would take the overnight train to Tokyo; all his worldly possessions carried in a slightly scarred black leather suitcase. Ryosako would be riding in second class; the first class had a dining car.

His stoic father could barely contain his emotions at the sight of his only son leaving the family's ancestral home, perhaps never to see him again. His mother openly wept, as did his younger sisters and other family members who dropped by to say their farewells and bid him a safe journey. They also wanted to wish him well, fearing it might be the last time they would see him in person too.

In Tokyo, he stayed at the home of his father's cousin in the Roppongi district of the city. He took a little time off to see some of the historic and commercial sites around the city, such as the moat-lined fortress Imperial Palace where the Emperor lived and the bustling commercial Ginza district.

The Tokyo Imperial Palace is the primary residence of the Emperor of Japan. It is a large park-like area located in the Chiyoda ward of Tokyo and contains buildings including the main palace, Kyūden - the private residences of the Imperial Family, an Archive, museums and administrative offices. It is built on the site of the old Edo Castle.

After the capitulation of the Shogunate and the Meiji Restoration, the inhabitants, including the Shogun Tokugawa Yoshinobu, were required to vacate the premises of the Edo Castle. Leaving the Kyoto Imperial Palace on

26 November 1868, the Emperor arrived at the Edo Castle in Tokyo and made it his new residence. In the Meiji era, most structures from the Edo Castle disappeared. Some were cleared to make way for other buildings while others were destroyed by earthquakes and fire.

Ryosako was completely at awe by the hustle and bustle of so many shoppers he encountered in the Ginza district which is not far from the Imperial Palace. It is a popular upscale shopping area of Tokyo, with numerous internationally renowned department stores, boutiques, and restaurants located in its vicinity. The Ginza was built upon a former swamp that was filled in during the 16th century. The name Ginza came after the establishment of a silver-coin mint established there in 1612, during the Edo period.

After a devastating fire in 1872 burned down most of the area, the Meiji government designated the Ginza area as a *"model of modernization."* The government planned the construction of fireproof brick buildings and larger, better streets connecting other districts of Tokyo. The area flourished as a symbol of *"civilization and enlightenment"*, thanks to the presence of newspapers and magazine companies, which helped spread the latest trends of the day. The area was also known for its window displays. Everyone visited, so the custom of *"killing time in Ginza"* developed strongly.

Although there was much to see at the Imperial Palace and the Ginza alone, Ryosako decided to spend more time than anywhere else at the venerated Yasukuni Shinto shrine. The elaborately carved structure was built in 1869 by the Emperor Meiji to commemorate the soldiers who fought and died to bring about his reign.

Yasukuni is a Shinto shrine. Various Shinto festivals are associated with it, particularly in the Spring and Autumn seasons when portable Mikoshi shrines are rounded about honoring the ancestral gods of Japan. A notable image of the shrine is the Japanese Imperial Chrysanthemum featured on the gate curtains leading into the shrine. The military government sought centralized state control over the memorialization of the war dead, giving Yasukuni a more central role. Enshrinements at Yasukuni were originally announced in the government's Official Gazette so that the souls could be treated as national heroes. Enshrinement at Yasukuni signified meaning and nobility to those who died for their country.

Japan's Emperor since 1912 was Taisho, son of Emperor Meiji. He died late in 1926, and a year later his son, Hirohito, ascended the throne. He had been brought up in the traditions of Japanese militarism. As a boy he admired his tutor, Count Maresuke Nogi, an old soldier and the headmaster of a school for the sons of the aristocracy. Nogi taught Hirohito the traditional spirit of Bushido and the Way of the Samurai Bushido, being a feudal-military code of chivalry that valued honor above life.

For Hirohito, Nogi embodied the spirit of Japanese religious faith, loyalty and bravery. Nogi's face and body bore traces of wounds from swords, arrows, bayonets, bullets and shrapnel. When Hirohito was twelve and his grandfather Emperor Meiji died. Nogi, seeing himself as a servant to Meiji, killed his wife and himself. Impressions of Nogi as representative of the Japanese spirit remained with Hirohito.

* * *

Ryosako's uncle helped him apply for his visa and other paperwork without which he would not be able to leave Japan and enter the United States. His ship sailed for San Francisco the following evening. The twenty-three days voyage was uneventful. Ryosako had been worried about seasickness but no storms interrupted the trip. Most of the passengers were Japanese like him, going to join relatives in America. As a passenger in second class, he couldn't really mingle with the few Westerners onboard, mostly Americans and a few Europeans. Also, he didn't think he would have been welcomed since they appeared to be affluent businessmen, diplomats, or members of the clergy. In any case, he didn't think that his command of the English language was adequate to carry a meaningful dialogue with any of them. So, during most of the voyage, he just read books on America history which he borrowed from the ship's small library, either in his small cabin or on the ship's lower promenade deck.

The highlight of the voyage was a two-day stopover for stores and other ship supplies in Honolulu. Hawaii was a fairly recent addition to American ownership. Ryosako carefully wrote a long letter home to his family and a shorter one to his Uncle in Tokyo thanking him for his hospitality during the layover. He was delighted to find a tiny Japanese mom and pop operated restaurant in downtown Honolulu. There, he had gyoza and soy sauce-based "shoyu" ramen noodle soup; he thought that was the best part of his trip crossing the Pacific.

After disembarking in San Francisco, he took out his carefully folded map, got his bearings and boarded a Greyhound bus. With a few hand gestures and a copy of the bus schedule, he took a front seat for the trip to

Salinas. The bus wasn't crowded. He ate a ham sandwich bought at a deli on Market Street, next to the bus station. The normal two-hour trip took longer because a stranded motorist had to be picked up and didn't have enough money for the fare. Contributions from the passengers readily solved that situation. The bus was an hour late but his Uncle Jiro was waiting patiently for him. Relieved to finally meet in person, they politely bowed to each other and then shook hands.

* * *

It was still dark outside that early fall morning in Salinas when Ryosako was awakened from dreaming about his trip to America by his Uncle's wife, Keiko. He had just arrived in Salinas the previous day and still thought his bed was rocking from the ocean waves. The rocking turned out to be a small earthquake, but he didn't think that much of the tremor; they were constant occurrences in Japan.

"Welcome to Salinas",

said his Aunt Keiko as she handed him a cup of green tea. She asked him to join her, their daughter Kazume, and his Uncle in the kitchen for a full American breakfast as soon as he was ready.

In the small kitchen, polite family introductions were made before serving breakfast. Ryosako was not used to having Canadian bacon, link sausages, scrambled eggs and pancakes for his first meal of the day. He was more inclined to the standard Japanese breakfast fare of steamed rice, pickled vegetables and small grilled fish like smelt. But, he realized he was in a new land now and promptly thanked his Aunt and Uncle for their hospitality. Uncle Jiro mentioned that it took a while for him to adjust to American way of eating too. Kazume added:

"When in Rome, do as the Romans do".

Aunt Keiko continued to tell a few more historical facts about his new residence:

"Salinas is Spanish for 'salt marsh' because there was a large slough that ran through the area when Spanish settlers first arrived. After Mexico seceded from Spain in 1822, Sausal and Nacional were among the first ranchos granted by the Mexican government.

It was on adjoining parts of these ranchos that 'Salinas City' was born after California became a territory of the United States."

Ryosako appreciated the early morning history lesson. At the same time, he also noticed that the sun was barely showing light through the rear kitchen window. His Aunt Keiko apologized for not letting him sleep longer. She had received a telegram a week ago from a relative in Nagaoka in Nigata prefecture back home. She was to expect today an important visitor who very much wanted to meet the entire family. She could not be told ahead of time who he was for security reasons. It sounded serious and the family was naturally concerned from the tone of the message.

Ryosako was helping put away some old empty farm containers in the barn when he was summoned by Kazume to join the family in the house. He hurried to change to his only pair of decent trousers and a wrinkled but clean shirt. He joined everyone in the front parlor where hot tea was being served. He bowed and greeted everyone present in a subdued tone:

"Ohayo Gozaimasu",

which meant *"Good Morning"*, before he took his seat.

The visitor was a middle-aged man who was short and well groomed. His Auntie noticed that his nails had been buffed. He wore a charcoal grey suit and his shoes were spit shined. But it was his educated manner of speech and military bearing that impressed Ryosako. Or was it perhaps, the chauffer-driven limousine waiting outside with the engine still running. By then, Ryosako had indeed thought that his Aunt had good reason to appear a bit worried about the telegram they received.

The gentleman apologized to the family for the secretive nature of his visit and the serious matter at hand. He needed help and could not trust anyone else except his family for support. The visitor didn't waste any additional time in directly asking them to look after an infant boy he was leaving to their care. He told them that they were his only family in America and that he could trust them to raise him well. He was almost overcome with emotion when, with his head bowed once more, said in a halting voice that his rank and position in Japanese society left him no other choice.

The visit wasn't long, lasting only about forty- five minutes, as it was pretty much a one-sided proposition. The Aunt and her daughter, Kasume, took the infant into the nearest bedroom, providing great care to see that he was comfortable. An ample supply of baby food, diapers, blankets, clothes and a crib were brought with the infant. The gentleman was pleased with the care the soon-to-be adoptive family showed the child. A quiet knock at the door followed. It was the chauffer informing the distinguished relative that it was time to leave and simultaneously handed him a large manila envelope. The visitor delicately handed it to Ryosako's Uncle and followed his chauffer out the door.

Uncle Jiro opened the metal tabs carefully and stared in amazement at the several rolls of green backs - American one hundred-dollar bills that were stuffed inside. Ryosako had never seen so much money, either Japanese or American. A short note inside written in Kanji accidently fell on the floor. When Ryosako picked it up to hand it to his Uncle, he noticed that the note said *"more to be sent in time."* He could only conclude that, contrary to what the visitor may have said earlier about his unannounced visit, he had, in fact, carefully planned it.

The infant was a beautiful child, fair in complexion, dark haired, but noticeably larger than most babies of Japanese parentage. He slept most of the remainder of that day while everyone went about their daily chores.

Aunt Keiko and Kasume were never far away from the child, with one of them rushing to his room whenever he made the faintest sound of discomfort. Occasionally, Uncle Jiro and Ryosako would wander in the house too, taking a break from tending to the chickens in their coop or the fruit trees and vegetables in the field surrounding the farm house. They all seemed to take delight about the newest member of the household.

During dinner later that day, it was Kasume who broke the silence as soon as the prayer meal was said and the servings of pork tonkatsu, sautéed yellow squash, and rice were passed around:

"I'd like to name the child after my late husband, Diego: he would be pleased if he were still here with us, I think."

Her mother replied:

"I think your late husband would be very pleased too",

as Uncle Jiro nodded his approval. Noticing Ryosako's curious look, Aunt Keiko added:

"You see, Kasume met Diego when they were still in high school. If it weren't for that fatal accident, he had on the coastal highway near Monterey during that terrible storm last year, he would be seated at this table with us today, telling jokes and enjoying hot sake with his dinner He was a character, a fine young man. He helped your Uncle

work the farm since he was a teenager when his family arrived here from Argentina."

Ryosako's curiosity naturally grew and asked:

"He was not Japanese, Auntie?"

"No, but that didn't bother him at all, nor the stares we got from some of the local town people whenever the family was seen together in public",

Kazume responded.

"Diego was color-blind as far as the color of a person's skin was concerned. He was comfortable talking to anyone, whoever they were, regardless of their religious or political beliefs, young and old, rich and poor alike.

Once, he saw some young teenagers trying to steal an Asian old man's bag of groceries, as he was walking along the side of the road on his way home from the store. He pulled over the side of the road and jump out of the car to help him. He chased them away and told them that if he ever saw them again in the neighborhood, he would cut off their testicles and feed them to the dogs.

I was more frightened of him than I was of the teenagers; I never saw him angrier in all the time I had known him. He told me later that he had hated bullies and punks all his life, because they always picked on people who couldn't defend themselves. We learned several days later that the elderly man was none other than his father-in-law's fellow migrant worker, Jesus Salvador. He emigrated from the

Philippines and married a beautiful Mexican woman from Los Angeles."

Then, the normally quiet Uncle Jiro joined in the conversation:

"I had seen him do the same sort of thing even when he was a teenager, you know, helping others in trouble. It happened right here on the farm too. A group of white men from nearby Watsonville were passing by on the way to town when they noticed our Japanese name on our fruit stand. They started yelling racial obscenities when they saw me come out to see what all the commotion was about."

"Wouldn't you believe it, Diego darted out of the barn, shotgun in hand yelling at them to leave immediately or he would blow their heads off. But what really

struck me as odd was what he actually said: 'Get off my family's property' to which one of the men replied; 'Boy, you're white like us'.

With no hesitation, he answered back:' I don't care, Sir; these folks are my family' I was so proud of that boy."

the Uncle added. Not quite finished saying her piece at the dinner table, Auntie Keiko also said:

"He was also tall, witty and blessed with handsome manly features which he must have inherited from his grandparents who were from the Basque region of northern Spain. The Ybarra family immigrated to Argentina. Diego's parents, in turn, left Argentina for California when he was only 7 years old at the turn of the

century. They don't live far from here; they miss their son a lot."

Uncle Jiro, who was now really absorbed in the dinner conversation, spoke up again:

"We'll give him two names, the first one, Diego, to honor the memory of his father and his Basque roots. The second, Masaharu, which was my father's name, shall reflect his Japanese ancestry. He will be raised as Kazume's child and christened Diego Masaharu Sawa Ybarra".

The family finished eating dinner; the men retired to the living room to finish off their bottle of sake, while the women washed and dried the dishes. Later, they joined the men in planning little Diego's forthcoming christening. The whole family was excited. The child was nearby in Kazume's room sound asleep.

* * *

A month flew by quickly and before anyone realized it, the special occasion was already underway. A banquet was held for little Diego right after he was christened at the Presbyterian community church in town. His Argentine grandparents, a few of their countrymen, and just about everyone in the Asian community of Salinas was also there, filling up the red brick building with the tall white spire. The civic hall, just a stone's throw from the church had been booked two weeks earlier for the huge gathering. The parking lot filled up quickly and so some of the late arrivals had to park on nearby residential streets.

The guests brought dishes from their native countries: Filipino adobo, Chinese egg noodles, and Argentine beef asado or grilled beef, in addition to Japanese dishes such as: shrimp tempura and Inari sushi. The Anglo and Hispanic parishioners, although fewer in number, brought desert: cake, pies, brownies and fresh fruit. Soda drinks, beer, and hard liquor were not in short supply either. A few of the men had to be restrained from drinking too much beer and sake. Overall, however, the guests were on their best behavior, even the toddlers who were occasionally yelled at by their parents to stop running aimlessly inside the hall. Most of the men took their meals outside in the church yard, where there were several picnic tables to be found.

The crowd was delighted to learn that the christened child was named after his father. No one had forgotten that tragic day when a young man's life was cut short. One of the worst Pacific storms to hit the valley in recent memory had ended tragically for one their own.

During the remainder of the festive afternoon, the women gossiped mostly about their neighbors, friends and fellow church members. Their teenage daughters openly flirted with their counterparts from high school. The older men consumed the liquor they brought, mingling war stories about the Great War, while the really old veterans reminisced about their participation in the Boxer Rebellion in China or in the Philippine Campaign at the beginning of the century. Everyone was having a great time! Charlie Watson, a survivor of the siege of the US Embassy in Peking, full of too much whisky, started sobbing about fellow Marines lost when the group of veterans decided to call it a day. The celebration came to an end.

VII - Outcast

"The world is a dangerous place, not because of those who do evil, but because of those who look on and do nothing."

Albert Einstein

Between 1925 and 1935, the Japanese population of the Salinas Valley grew to an estimated 250 families, with 200 in the vicinity of Salinas, 30 around Chualar and 25 in and around Castroville. During these years Castroville had both a small Chinatown and Japan town.

The Issei or first-generation Japanese had already established a Japanese School at the Salinas Buddhist Temple. In the mid-1930s, they also set up branches in Chualar and Castroville to serve the growing number of Nisei, second generation, reaching school age. In 1935, a corporation named "The Buddhist Church of Castroville" purchased the entire block bounded by Geil, Pajaro, Seymour, and Union streets. Because of California's Alien Laws, the corporation was led by Nisei signing the original deed.

Not long afterward, the community began building the small Japanese school building on the southwest corner of the property, and, for the next six years, many of the Nisei children living in and around Castroville attended the school. Classes were held in the afternoons beginning at 3:00 PM for two hours with another half-day on Saturdays. The curriculum centered on the Japanese language, with other instruction covering Japanese cultural practices.

The Issei parents were hoping that their children might learn some of the Japanese traditions in this school while learning about America in public school. The teachers were hired by the Salinas Buddhist Temple, and compensated through the tuition paid by the Issei parents. All the Japanese Schools closed immediately following the bombing of Pearl Harbor on December 7, 1941.

* * *

Diego attended the public schools in Salinas. The solid brick buildings were stifling during the warm weather months. The long halls always smelled of floor wax. Diego loved the library, even though hours were limited. The librarian always complained that re-shelving books was such a pain. Fortunately, she had already retired.

Diego especially loved his math classes under Mr. Jorgensen, who had an innate sense of how to explain background concepts. This was very useful in geometry. The chalk dust also made him sneeze and so the students would wait for him to get out his large handkerchief to blow his nose before proceeding to the next proof. The school also had a small gym which was made of brick too and was just as hot and stuffy. Diego didn't care for indoor basketball for that reason. He preferred to play outdoors where you could breathe. And then, of course, football was his favorite. Diego was an outstanding student, excelling both in academics and sports in elementary and high school. But his grandparents also made sure that he received extra schooling in Japanese history and culture including reading and writing kanji and hiragana.

A phonetic lettering system, literally meaning *"ordinary"* or *"simple"* kana, hiragana is one of the three main components of the Japanese writing system, along with Katakana, Kanji, and in some cases Romaji or Latin Script. It is used to write Okurigana or kana suffixes following a kanji root to inflect verbs and adjectives, various grammatical and function words. These also include particles, as well as miscellaneous other native words for which there are no kanji or whose kanji form is obscure or too formal for the writing purpose. Words that do have common kanji renditions may also sometimes be written instead in hiragana to impart an informal feel.

By the same token, Katakana is another component of the Japanese writing system just like Hiragana, Kanji, and Romaji. Katakana means "fragmentary kana", as its characters are derived from components of more complex kanji. Katakana, like Hiragana is a kana or character system. With minor exceptions, each syllable is represented by one character, or kana. Each kana is either a vowel such as "a"; a consonant followed by a vowel such as "ka"; or "n", or a nasal sonorant.

In contrast to Hiragana, which is used for Japanese words not covered by Kanji and for grammatical inflections, Katakana usage is quite similar to italics in English. Specifically, it is used for transcription of foreign language words into Japanese; for technical and scientific terms; and for names of plants, animals, minerals, and often Japanese companies. Katakana is characterized by short, straight strokes and sharp corners.

The Japanese school was in Castroville, a small community just a few miles north of Salinas. Since the family farm was almost mid-point between the two communities, it didn't take that much time to get there. A family member, usually his elder cousin Ryosako, drove Diego there and back three times a week. Sometimes, his mother, Kazume took over the job, when Ryosako was busy with either farm chores or volunteering as an orderly at the infirmary in town.

Diego was popular with both his teachers and fellow students and so his family was naturally very proud of him. They often mused about he cried so much at his christening and how that was taken to be a sign of good fortune, which was to follow him for the rest of his life.

But as young Diego later found out, that was not always true in real life.

When he was in the 5th grade, he was paddle boarded by the school principal because he got into a minor fracas with another student. He didn't start the fight, so he got paddled only once while the other student received two for instigating the fight. Still, Diego thought it was unfair that he was even punished. After all, he was only defending himself. The boyhood experience stuck in his mind all through his adult life.

While in high school, he became fond of a girl in his math class. But she rejected his overtures and told him that it was inappropriate for them to go out together because of their different racial backgrounds. Her parents would not permit them to go out together. Diego took it very hard initially but eventually got over it, finding some solace in the adage that after all:

"No one can choose their parents."

But, bouncing back and moving forward instead of dwelling on the past or "crying over spilled milk" was a trait that was to remain one of the cornerstones of his character for the rest of his life. He viewed in positive terms any adversity he faced, determined to learn from it and better himself from each episode.

The children of Japanese immigrants like Diego's stepmother struggled to understand their place in American society during the first half of the 20th century. However, for the second generation Japanese or Nisei, their experience was unique because of anti-Asian sentiment in California. During the Depression era of the 1930s', Japanese-Americans had the largest number of American born children in the U.S. among Asian-American groups. Like the Chinese and Filipinos, they faced much of the same discrimination and severe immigration restrictions.

Beginning in 1882, the federal government passed a series of Chinese exclusion laws that made Chinese migration into America illegal. With the exception of merchants, diplomats, and students, no Chinese were allowed to enter America. Congress passed these exclusion laws in response to a growing tide of working-class anger over Chinese labor in California. With a valuable source of cheap labor gone, American employers began recruiting labor from Japan to work in California's growing farms, mines, and factories.

Threatened California workers, particularly San Franciscans, reacted angrily to what they saw as yet another wave of cheap Asian labor. However, by the early 20th century Japan had become a rising world power. Banning the Japanese, as had been done with the Chinese would have made tense relations with Japan even worse. President Theodore Roosevelt moved quickly to halt Japanese immigration without upsetting U.S.-Japanese relations.

Roosevelt successfully quelled Californians' demands and averted offending Japan through the 1907-1908 Gentleman's Agreement, a series of informal letters between American and Japanese leaders. This agreement virtually halted all Japanese contract labor to America. However, the Agreement did allow the continuation of the picture bride system. In the early 20th century, the advent of photography modernized traditional arranged marriages in Asia. Photographs and letters replaced face-to-face meetings between families and matchmakers. For the first time, prospective couples living in different parts of Japan could be introduced.

Japanese immigrants residing in California also took full advantage of the new technology and the stipulation in the Gentlemen's Agreement that allowed them to bring wives to America. By 1940, approximately 61% of the state's Japanese-American community was American born, or Nisei. In comparison, American born Chinese comprised 52% of the Chinese American community by 1940.

For Nisei, the question of identity became progressively more difficult to handle. By the mid-1930s, the Japanese- Americans, 70% of which lived in California, were in a state of heightened alert. Anti-Japanese sentiment was rising to dangerously new levels with Japan's increasing expansion in Asia. Little Tokyos in Los Angeles, San Francisco, and other West Coast cities were also dying. While the Nisei wanted to spend their money in fancy downtown department stores, not in Little Tokyos, they still depended on them for jobs.

On the other hand, racism made it extremely difficult for Nisei to find jobs outside the ethnic economy, even with degrees from schools like UCLA and UC Berkeley. The only work many Nisei could find was on their parents' farms or in Little Tokyo stores. With no new immigration since the 1924 National Origins Act, no one was shopping in Little Tokyo anymore. Both generations knew that if they did not revitalize the ethnic economy, the effects would be disastrous.

* * *

In his teens, Diego spent a lot of time hanging out with Ryosako, his older cousin, doing chores together on the family farm. Diego sometimes helped with the laundry, using a wringer washing machine on the back porch and hanging bed sheets to dry. Ryosako, however, was also interested in the medical field. It had been in his blood since he was a boy growing up in his village in Japan. Diego would occasionally accompany him while he delivered medical supplies or transported patients to and from the hospital in town. But, his interest in that sort of work stopped with transporting patients because the sight of sickly patients or even blood being drawn always made him feel nauseous.

The small stucco-sided hospital had fewer than 30 inpatient beds. There were no private rooms, except for the extremely ill; they needed to be near the nurse's station. The wards were divided into male and female sections. Heavy canvas draperies separated the patients when privacy was a concern. The smell of disinfectant was strong. There were only two doctors and they were both men. All of the nurses were women.

* * *

Not to be overlooked, Diego's Argentine grandparents on his father's side also took great care to see that their grandson was knowledgeable of his Spanish heritage. His grandfather, Pedro Ybarra, taught him both Castilian and American Spanish. The former is one of the five languages of Spain. The others are Basque, Galician, Catalan, and Aranese.

Castilian Spanish is the official national language of Spain, and so-named for its roots in the region of Castile. Castilian Spanish was brought to the New World through the colonization efforts of the Spanish government. Over time, it evolved into Latin American Spanish and contains various features that distinguish it from European Spanish. The terms Castilian Spanish or Castellano are often used to draw a distinction between the Spanish spoken in Spain or Peninsular Spanish and Latin American Spanish. While there is no generic form of Latin American Spanish, many countries share several features of pronunciation, vocabulary and grammar that set it apart from Castilian Spanish. Despite the differences, the beauty of Spanish is that regardless of the dialect that one speaks, its speakers can communicate with minimal difficulties.

Diego also studied the history of Argentina and its culture. He spent weekends and sometimes entire summers with his grandparents from Argentina at their ranch in Monterey, where he learned to ride, rope, and break horses among other things.

The ranch house was built Spanish style. With stucco sides, orange red tile roofing, and a trickling fountain in front. Fruit trees and flowering vines gave the place a colorful painting look. The inside of the house was cool in the summer as the roof eaves shaded the living quarters. The tile floors were easy to keep clean, his grandmother said. The house had four working fireplaces, one in the living room and one in each of the three bedrooms. The living room fireplace had distinctive tile work done, which Diego especially liked.

The ranch was just off Highway 1. Older residents still referred to it as the King's Highway, El Camino Real, harking back to that period in the past, when California used to belong to Spain. Occasionally, his grandparents reminded him that his father lost his life in a terrible storm on Highway 1 in 1920, the same year he was born.

Diego was fascinated with the Argentine family stories handed down from one generation to the next when he was growing up. The life of the *"gaucho"*, the Argentine cowboy, left him with memorable impressions. During the annual July 4th 'asado' or barbecue family celebrations, a young cow, with its hide still intact, was grilled all day long in an open pit full of hot coals. His grandfather told him that:

"In the Pampas region of Argentina not too long ago, when there were no fences and no dividers between ranches, cattle used to move freely on open lands. The hired hands or Gauchos tended the cattle and performed other duties on horseback. They prepared 'Asado con Cuero', by killing a whole young cow and roasting it with the hide on.

A lot of firewood was initially burned to coals to prevent embers from producing any flames when the meat was placed over it on a large metal grill. The temperature was set high initially and then lowered afterwards. They flavored the meat with 'salumeria', a water-based sauce consisting mainly of salt, garlic, and pepper while it was cooking, with the bony side being cooked first.

Then, after several hours when the meat was sufficiently roasted, the gauchos used their large knives and cut individual servings of un-skinned meat for the hungry guests. The feast lasted the whole day, from sun up till late in the day. Everyone filled their bellies and had a wonderful time!"

While the beef asado was slowly roasting, couples both old and young, danced to the tango music blaring in the background. They rested only briefly to partake of *"mate"*, a green tea like mixture of dried leaves of yerba mate in hot water.

Counterclockwise, the parties whirled around the outside of a hastily improvised dance area. They engaged in a closed embrace in which the connection is chest to chest, each dancer transmitting a feeling of the music to their respective partner, just as they did back in the old country. Mesmerized by the melodic sounds of the musicians' bandoneon and violin, Diego learned to tango at a very young age. He was to cherish those happy times later in adulthood.

* * *

When he wasn’t attending public school or Japanese language classes, Diego often went to the library in downtown Salinas with Ryosako because it had more books to choose from than his high school. Both immersed themselves with national and world events including the local news to pass the time away. The library newspapers and magazines certainly provided wider in-depth coverage of the national news than the abbreviated radio reports they got at home. Diego took particular delight in reading every new issue of the National Geographic magazine. He enjoyed glossing over the stunning color photographs of exotic and faraway places like Normandy, a coastal province on the English Channel in France, the Taj Mahal in India, or the Great Wall in China. He fantasized seeing all of them when he grew up.

The library visits were also a convenient excuse to grab a greasy burger in town and socialize with the young girls who hung out there. Hamburgers were a welcomed change from the *"gohan"* or rice, fish and vegetable meals they ate at home. Town outings were a nice change of pace from the daily routine chores of life on the farm for the two young men. However, it was also during these library excursions into town that he learned about pressing local socio-economic and political problems.

He read about the violent farm labor disputes in the Salinas valley dating back to the 1880s. He also learned about the influx of unwelcomed *"Dust Bowl"* immigrants from the Midwest, followed later by the racial strife between local white residents and newly-arrived migrant laborers from the Philippines and Mexico.

The newspaper accounts and journals in the library validated the stories he had, from time to time, heard from his friends and family. For instance, contrary to the popular opinion of the time, the Dust Bowl didn't just happen overnight as he and Ryosako later found out. In fact, it had been taking place for at least a decade for reasons which just seemed pre-destined to arrive together at the same time.

Following the relative prosperity of the post-World War I era, the prices of farm crops rose and fell with good rain. During the same period, the government in Washington encouraged the farmers to plant more. But this led to over planting of crops exacerbated by acquisition of new land to plant more crops. Add to this, the easy availability of credit to buy equipment. Before you knew it, those same farmers had already put them to use tearing up land even faster. It didn't end there. The farmers didn’t rotate their crops either nor did they leave areas of native grasses. They just dug up everything leaving the ground upside down with the native grasses’ underneath and the dirt on top. It was all right as long as good rain was plentiful, which for the record later turned out to be a climate aberration. But when there was only normal low rainfall; well, the bare soil dried up and then the strong winds came.

The Dust Bowl in the Midwest began sending migrants to California in 1934. There was little housing in rural areas for them and *"Hoovervilles"* sprung up. So, the government began in the summer of 1935, to build migrant labor camps. It was reasoned that if government could not keep people out of the state, then it should do what it could to aid needy residents. Instead of the *"pioneer tradition"* of giving the poor food and sending them on their way, shelters were built that provided food, medical care, and counseling in exchange for one to three hours of work or community service.

Federal government camps were seen by most as the places in which migrants could be turned into *"class-conscious"* agricultural laborers. Ironically, however, these same migrants tried to avoid permanent employment as wage laborers by saving enough to become small farmers in their own right. Of course, back then, Blacks and Mexicans were often excluded from these same camps.

It was against this backdrop that America also contended with the fear of communism and issues of racial justice, that in 1938, the Pulitzer Prize and Nobel Prize winning author, John Steinbeck, wrote his novel *"The Grapes of Wrath."* Set in California's Salinas Valley, the story took place during the Great Depression. Steinbeck's novel opened with the Joad family being pushed off their farm in eastern Oklahoma, and follows the family west for 1,200 miles on Route 66 through Texas, New Mexico, and Arizona to California.

The Dust Bowl migrant characters in the novel captured the imagination of many Americans in part because readers could easily identify with them. But the naysayers or those who thought otherwise, alleged that John Steinbeck shrewdly used the plight of the migrants to urge changes in California's rural economy, to either: accept a system of factory farms and regulate the farm labor market, or to break up big California farms and give land to the workers. Most folks believed, however, that the farm worker strikes were simply protests over low wages, especially when the farmers failed to raise wages as their own prices rose because of government farm subsidies.

During the 1930s, it is estimated that 1.3 million Americans from the Midwest and Southwest migrated to California, whose population then was 5.7 million. When the Okies and Arkies arrived, the stage was set for physical and ideological conflicts over how to deal with seasonal farm labor. The newly arrived migrants in California needed help in making the transition from the non-irrigated cotton and grain farming of the Midwest to irrigated fruit and vegetable farming in California. And so, camps and cooperative were formed to train the newcomers in the vagaries of California agriculture. In the fall of 1931 alone, migrants were arriving in the state at the rate of 1,200 to 1,500 a day, an annual rate of almost 500,000.

In the Salinas Valley, agriculture was dominated by large collective farms, or *"farm factories,"* owned by wealthy landowners and banks. Small farms of a few hundred acres were relatively scarce. The farm factories employed hundreds of workers, many of whom were migrants. Some growers, including the 4,000-acre Tagus Ranch, offered free or low-cost housing as well as on-farm schools and stores for workers. But certain segments of the population disapproved or thought on-farm housing and other services were feudalistic. They lulled workers into fear of ever leaving the ranch, much less even consider other jobs because they would lose their housing. At these large farms, low wages for picking fruit and vegetables often led to economic unrest. For instance, in September 1936, thousands of lettuce workers in the Salinas Valley went on strike over such low wages.

Beside the problems brought about by the arrival of the Dust Bowl migrants, California was also beset by a growing Asian population. The Salinas valley faced ongoing challenges in the wake of California's Asian exclusion laws. When thousands of Chinese and Japanese workers were brought to work in the fruit orchards and sugar beet fields during the late 1800s, they became the first farm workers to form associations and strike for improved wages and conditions. But their victories were short-lived. The growers played them off against whites and other immigrant workers, especially during the depression years of the 1870's and early 1900's by blaming them for taking away jobs from *"Americans"*.

Racist laws were passed excluding the Chinese in 1882 and Japanese in 1920 from the

U.S. Shortly thereafter, waves of farmers from Oklahoma, Arkansas, and Texas who were displaced by the Great Depression came to California and joined the Mexicans and Filipinos already employed on the factory farms of the large grower-shippers.

As the Depression deepened, the growers slashed wages and proceeded to lay off workers. Between 1929 and 1933, wages dropped from $3.50 to $1.90 a day and a 3-year residency requirement disqualified most farm workers from any government relief. Left with no choice, the farm workers walked out of the fields telling the growers, "You can pick your own crops for $1.75 a day!" The biggest strike took place in October 1933 among cotton workers in the Central Valley, where wages in cotton had fallen from $1 to 40 cents per 100 lbs. picked.

Over 1800 workers walked out, three-fourths of whom were Mexican while the remaining 1/4 were white and black. Many of the strikes were led by the Cannery and Agricultural Workers Industrial Union (CAWIU), whose leaders included communists and other progressive workers.

Another major change in agriculture took place when sugar beets and beans gave way to the *"green gold"* of lettuce. The development of ice bunkered railroad cars made it possible to ship fresh produce nationwide and lettuce replaced the sugar beet as the Salinas Valley mainstay, although other row crops were grown as well, including the artichoke. Also, as the Japanese labor force had succeeded the Chinese with the advent of the sugar beet, so now the Filipinos replaced the Japanese as the labor force for new row crops.

After World War I, California growers began importing farm workers from the Philippines, which the U.S. had seized after a war with Spain in 1898. But laws were passed forbidding Filipino women from entering the U.S and in many rural towns it was a crime for Filipino men to associate with women of other races. The growers hoped to keep their expenses down by employing a work force of single men. But in the early 1930s, the Filipino workers responded by organizing into associations which led some powerful strikes.

A close-knit people by national character, the Filipinos wasted little time in forming "local barangays". This was a functional social concept which predates western influence and is the backbone of Filipino community action. Initiated in 1906 as the Caballeros de Dimas-alang, a Salinas lodge was formed in 1920 with its center in the Filipino community church. The Caballeros' organization funded a newspaper in

1928, the Pilipino Independent News, which in 1930 became the oldest continuing Filipino newspaper in the United States. Then, just prior to World War II another newspaper, the Philippines Mail, became a rallying point of Filipino opinion and inspiration. It took on such national issues as the Federal Repatriation Act of 1932 and strongly supported the position of the Filipino laborer during their strike against agri-industrial business in 1934.

Lobby groups in California led by American laborers had lobbied to bar Filipinos from the U.S., which was similar to the exclusion policy against the Chinese and Japanese. In 1929, the state legislature passed a resolution calling for a congressional enactment to restrict Filipino immigration. At the same time, there were persistent calls for the repatriation of the Filipinos. The Great Depression exacerbated race relations and provided more compelling reasons to restrict

Filipino migration. In 1935, the U.S Congress passed the Repatriation Act calling for Filipino repatriation but most Filipinos chose to remain in California and only a couple of thousand ended up returning home to the Philippines.

Racial violence erupted in communities with a sizable number of Filipinos. The first race riot occurred in Exeter, California, on the night of October 24, 1929 after white Americans were displaced by Filipinos in harvesting kadota figs and emperor grapes. A mob of 300 men stormed a Filipino camp, stoned and clubbed about 50 Filipinos. About 200 were driven out of the district altogether. The most explosive riot occurred in Watsonville where Filipinos had been constantly harassed since their first arrival.

On January 11, 1930, a small Filipino club leased a dance hall in Palm Beach. The thought of Filipinos dancing with white women angered Watsonville citizens. On January 20, 1930, about 200 Americans hunted Filipinos on the streets, and on the following day, the dance hall was raided. Two days later, Filipinos were beaten and one was killed by a mob of 500 white Americans who also destroyed the Filipino quarters.

* * *

Diego's cousin, Ryosako had a couple of close friends in town: Cesar Bautista, a young man of Filipino ancestry and Danny Chan, whose parents emigrated from Hong Kong when he was still a small boy. They had both worked at the family farm after school and on weekends during the fruit and vegetable harvest season, since they were young teenagers. They were all like older brothers to the younger Diego. They taught him the routine farm chores of feeding the livestock, fertilizing the crops and maintaining the farm equipment and vehicles. Of course, being young men in the prime of their youth, they also availed themselves of certain manly activities such as boxing, and charming the local girls at neighborhood dances, all of which naturally delighted the youthful and inquisitive Diego.

The history of racial violence in Salinas was more than just a series of stories about the labor problems in the Valley for Diego personally. He grew up on his Grandfather Jiro's farm working alongside Ryosako, planting and harvesting seasonal crops. Cesar's family and their fellow Filipino neighbors were always there ready to lend a hand, whenever they were needed. Grandfather Jiro thought well of them. As fellow Asians, they were reliable, honest and hard working.

Just before the outbreak of WW ll, it was grandfather Jiro who brokered a marriage between Cesar and the daughter of one of his

Japanese associates from nearby Castroville. Diego looked up to Cesar as well and considered him more like an older brother than just a family friend. Of course, he always enjoyed eating "pancit", a traditional Filipino pan-fried noodle dish, whenever Cesar's mom made it for him. It went a long way towards cementing their close friendship.

VIII - War & Conflict

"Government even in its best state, is but a necessary evil."

Thomas Paine

Salinas and Monterey counties had large populations of Japanese-American farmers, fishermen and merchants. Within weeks of Pearl Harbor, President Franklin D. Roosevelt issued Executive Order 9066 on February 19, 1942, authorizing the relocation of West Coast Japanese Americans.

With their removal from the West Coast, the Japanese had to face the losses associated with their hard work in developing the land. Those fortunate enough to own their land would have to find reliable renters to care for their property. Families left their homes, farms and businesses and were ordered into primitive shelters at fairgrounds and horse racing tracks, including the Salinas Rodeo Grounds. Vast internment camps were later constructed throughout the West to house them all, upwards of 120,000 people, most of them U.S. citizens.

In 1943, when the Nisei, who were second-generation American born Japanese, were finally allowed to enlist in the US military, thousands joined up, and with the 100th Battalion from Hawaii formed the 442nd Regimental Combat Team. The 442nd went into action north of Rome in 1944. By the end of the war, the regiment's soldiers had earned over 18,000 medals, including seven Presidential Unit Citations, 21 Medals of Honor and over 9,000 Purple Hearts.

The Nisei veterans did not set out to be heroes. Some had enlisted or were drafted into the military before the U.S. went to war. They joined the crowds of patriotic young men lining up to enlist on Dec. 7, 1941 when they learned Pearl Harbor had been attacked. That was when they were told they were not wanted, not allowed to enlist or be drafted.

* * *

The war in Europe had been raging for over two years. Hitler's armies were already Masters of the European continent and were now knocking on the doorsteps of Moscow. In Asia the Japanese had wreaked havoc in China even longer. In the 1930s, Japanese political and intellectual thinking gradually shifted from economic liberalism toward more economic control under state management. There were many reasons for this, including: influence of Marxism, apparent success of USSR, Showa Depression, the idea that deflation was worsened by excess competition and disappointment with politicians and political parties. Many considered that the days of the US style free market economy were over and from now on, state control and industrial monopoly would strengthen the competitiveness of the national economy.

Military and right-wing movements emerged. In economic despair, much blame was placed on party governments and their policies. Even ordinary people, who normally hated militarism, were disappointed with the performance of party governments and became more sympathetic to the military and nationalists. Another aim of the military and right-wing groups was active military expansion. While there were earlier calls for economic planning before the war, the Japanese economy basically remained market-oriented until 1936. But with the outbreak of the Japan-China War in 1937, the economy was completely transformed for war execution. One by one, new measures were introduced to control and mobilize people, enterprises and resources. Most Japanese firms remained privately-owned but were heavily regulated to contribute to the war effort.

Of course, this was old news to Diego's family and most of America. Diego was already in his late teens by this time and was fully aware of the uncertain future that lay before him. The anxiety was heightened by the constant media barrage of the inevitable entry of America in the war against Germany. Just like many young men his age, he was sure he would join the fighting when it broke out. However, like most residents on the West coast, he wasn't particularly worried about the war coming to California's shores any time soon.

Hitler and his Nazi hordes were foremost in the minds of everyone in the Valley, and they were certain that if and when war broke out, it would take place back East first. Grandpa Jiro had his doubts, however. In private conversations with Reverend Yutaka Tomonaga and other leading parishioners about the likelihood of open hostility between Japan and America, he had expressed a different view. The embargo on the export of oil to Japan which President Roosevelt had imposed several months earlier was what made him switch his mind.

It was just another early Sunday afternoon, when the elderly Reverend Tomonaga could be seen standing outside the church door entrance after conducting services, just as he has done every weekend as far back as anyone could remember. Without skipping anyone, he would cheerfully shake the hands of each parishioner on their way out. Occasionally, he would comment about the lovely weather for the picnic which was held afterwards in the park, adjacent to the church, depending on the weather conditions. In turn, his parishioners would briefly talk about the potluck dishes they brought with them that day. Others simply looked forward to enjoying a lazy game of softball or just catching up with the local gossip in the tightly knit community. This time, however, it was early December and the Reverend was pleased to see that almost everyone in his parish was present for the Sunday services. He knew from his long service in the community that they felt compelled to attend services during this time of the year, with the Christmas season fast approaching.

Diego's family was in full attendance, including his Argentine grandparents. Their Chinese, Filipino, and Mexican friends and neighbors were there too. They were all trustworthy and reliable friends who provided needed seasonal help during the crop harvests. This was particularly true during those turbulent years of labor unrest and strikes by migrant farm laborers in the Salinas valley during the 1930s. Diego's grandfather witnessed those events firsthand and often recounted them to the family over the dinner table. Lawful or not, labor problems affected the output of both the large agricultural farms and the independently owned smaller ones like the one belonging to him.

People of all ages, young and old, children with their parents, friends and relatives, could be seen enjoying themselves at the picnic area. While most were seated at the tables poised to sample every plate that was being passed around, others were still milling around the park looking for the best spots to seat themselves, perhaps to be nearer friends or family. In the center of the picnic grounds, four plank-top tables were purposely set aside and stacked with all of the dishes that were brought that day. Diego was always awed by the variety of food available. He was standing in line waiting his turn to fill his plate when he noticed his mother, Kazume, walking toward him:

"It's been almost 18 years now, Diego, but I remember your christening being as festive as the picnic we're having today."

"You're kidding, Mom",

he replied.

"Not at all, Son; I was there!"
said a balding elderly man standing in line behind Diego. His Mom replied:

"Well, OK; perhaps I exaggerated a little, but I recall at least two or three picnic tables full of food and a crowd as large as the one we have here today."

By that time, everyone in line had also heard the ongoing small talk and joined in the conversation before Diego could utter another word. Feeling left out of the conversation, he quietly drifted towards another group. This time, he joined Cesar and Ryosako who was talking about Aikido, a relatively new form of Jujitsu based martial arts that he had studied in Japan before immigrating to America. This was more to Diego's liking since he routinely trained with them after during the week back on the farm.

One of the younger men in the crowd asked:

"It's a relatively new form of martial arts, isn't it? Who developed it and how is it different from other martial arts?"

Ryosako had to clear his throat before replying to what was obviously a loaded question.

"Well, I guess you could say that if you compare it to, for example, Jujitsu or

Judo. First, let me say that Aikido was introduced by Morihei Ueshiba who envisioned it as an expression of his personal philosophy of universal peace and reconciliation. It was developed during the late 1920s through the synthesis of the older martial arts that he had studied.

The core martial art from which Aikido is derived is Daito-ryu aiki-jujutsu. The art of Daito-ryu is the primary technical influence on Aikido. Along with empty-handed throwing and joint-locking techniques, Ueshiba incorporated training movements with weapons, such as those for the spear (Yari), and short staff (Jo). However, Aikido derives much of its technical structure from the art of swordsmanship (kenjutsu)."

Another young man asked:

"Where did all this take place?"

Ryosako had to clear his throat once more and gladly took a sip of soda someone handed him. He realized he had a longer story to tell about the Aikido founder:

"Sensei Ueshiba moved to Hokkaido in 1912, and began studying under Takeda Sokaku in 1915. His official association with Daito-ryu continued until 1937. However, during the latter part of that period, Ueshiba had already begun to distance himself from Takeda and the Daito-ryu. At that time Ueshiba was referring to his martial art as "Aiki Budo". It is unclear exactly when Ueshiba began using the name "Aikido", but it became the official name of the art in 1942 when the Greater Japan Martial Virtue Society (Dai Nippon Butoku was engaged in a

government sponsored reorganization and centralization of Japanese martial arts.

After Ueshiba left Hokkaido in 1919, he met and was profoundly influenced by Onisaburo Deguchi, the spiritual leader of the Omoto-kyo religion (a neo-Shinto movement). One of the primary features of Omoto-kyo is its emphasis on the attainment of utopia during one's life. This was a great influence on Ueshiba's martial arts philosophy of extending love and compassion especially to those who seek to harm others. Aikido demonstrates this philosophy in its emphasis on mastering martial arts so that one may receive an attack and harmlessly redirect it. In an ideal resolution, not only is the receiver unharmed, but so is the attacker.

In addition to the effect on his spiritual growth, the connection with Deguchi gave

Ueshiba entry to elite political and military circles as a martial artist. As a result of this exposure, he was able to attract not only financial backing but also gifted students."

Diego thought about stepping in to relieve his cousin from what was turning into a lengthy lecture. Actually, he wanted to demonstrate some basic hand techniques when two young boys suddenly came out of nowhere shouting:

"The Japanese bombed Hawaii; the Japanese bombed Hawaii."

The crowd appeared stunned; some thought it was a prank. They saw the boys waving everyone to come over to where they were. When they heard the horrible news over a national broadcast station, they realized the serious gravity of the event. The young men with the radio, it turned out, were Ryosako and

Cesar Bautista. They had been listening to a baseball game when it was suddenly interrupted by the news of the sneak attack on the naval base at Pearl Harbor in the Hawaiian Islands. It was almost noon when the news was broadcasted to the American public via radio bulletins.

The news of the Japanese attack on American territory left the crowd speechless. Just minutes ago, they were celebrating the start of the holiday season and now they were left staring at each other in utter disbelief. Some remarked that the war was supposed to begin back East; after all, it had already been raging in Europe for almost two years. Others were more vocal about the treacherous manner in which Japan had started the war and made no effort to hide their anger at those *"sneaky Japs"*, ignoring the presence of so many Americans of Japanese descent among them at the church picnic.

Wasting no time following the aftermath of the news broadcast, the parishioners calmly gathered and wrapped the left-over food, drinks and plates. A few elderly women cried openly. The men loaded the stuff in their vehicles. Meanwhile, Reverend Tomonaga quietly moved about them, reassuring everyone that everything will be all right because God will not abandon his flock. He tried very hard to comfort those who were visibly upset. With others though, it was a vain effort. They vowed that the country would now join in the fight and that they will be ready to repel a similar attack on the West Coast.

* * *

The normally festive short drive back to the family farm from Sunday morning services always has the entire family looking forward to a carefree and relaxing afternoon. But with the

Pearl Harbor attack, the mood was understandably different.

Diego noticed that his grandfather Jiro was visibly quiet. Usually, he would be whistling a tune while driving with one hand on the wheel and the other on the car door. His grandmother had not stopped crying since they left the picnic grounds. She was consoled by Kazume. Ryosaku simply stared outside the car window as they drove by the fruit orchards on the way home. It seemed to take forever to get back to the farm from Sunday service that day. When they finally arrived, Diego and Ryosako unloaded the food and drinks while Kazume helped grandma into the house. Grandpa remained seated inside the car until everyone got out. Then, he parked it inside the garage. The news of the Pearl Harbor attack continued to be broadcasted on the radio the rest of that afternoon.

President Roosevelt delivered a speech to Congress declaring war on Japan the next day, calling the attack by their naval and air forces a surprise offensive and premeditated invasion. The declaration of war sent a shockwave across the nation and resulted in a tremendous influx of young volunteers into the U.S. Armed Forces in the weeks which followed. The Pearl Harbor bombing united the nation behind the President and effectively ended all isolationist sentiment in the country.

A week later, as the entire family was preparing to have Sunday dinner, they learned that the Japanese government had actually experienced *"bureaucratic"* delays in trying to issue a formal declaration of war with the United States. These prevented the Japanese diplomats from presenting their country's declaration of war to Secretary of State, Cordell Hull, until 2:30 PM in Washington, D.C. This was about the same time as the first reports of the air raid at Pearl Harbor were being read by the Secretary. Shortly thereafter, the Federal government swiftly moved to begin solving the *"Japanese problem"* on the West Coast of the United States, directing the FBI to arrest selected *"enemy aliens"* who were of Japanese descent. California pressed the Federal authorities for action because it was alarmed about potential subversive activities by people of Japanese ancestry within its borders.

In Salinas, and other communities in California with a sizable Asian population, a sinister atmosphere of gloom and anger soon settled in the valley. In fact, anyone living in the United States, especially on the West Coast, who even remotely looked Japanese was viewed with suspicion of being an enemy collaborator. That included the Chinese and Filipinos since:

"they all looked alike",

to most white Americans. This prejudice was often displayed by ordinary citizens, who vent their anger in public. It persisted in the weeks and months which followed the attack at Pearl Harbor, when America's possessions in the Pacific: Wake Island, Guam, and the Philippines were also overtaken. The British surrender of Hong Kong and Singapore at around the same time period didn't help to diffuse the situation. Some of the media blamed the military and government in general in adding to the *"yellow horde"* hysteria which actually began years earlier when Japan invaded Manchuria and China in 1939.

After the Pearl Harbor attack on December 7, 1941, President Roosevelt was pressured by the public at large to sign an Executive Order in February, which authorized the Secretary of War to designate military commanders to prescribe military areas and to exclude *"any or all persons"* from such areas. The order also authorized the construction of what would later be called *"relocation centers"* by the War Relocation Authority (WRA) to house those who were to be excluded. And so, in April 1942, Lt. General John L. Dewitt, Western Defense Commander, ordered the internment of Japanese Americans on the West Coast.

Over 110,000, two-thirds of whom were native-born American citizens, with the rest prevented from becoming citizens by federal law, were imprisoned in ten relocation centers located far inland and away from the coast. Proclamations were issued to evacuate five classes of aliens and citizens; namely: those suspected of sabotage or subversive activity, Japanese aliens, Japanese-Americans, German aliens, and Italian aliens. German and Italian aliens who had children in the US armed forces were not required to move.

* * *

Diego immediately noticed that something was wrong when he entered the house with Ryosaku to have lunch with the rest of the family. It was almost half past noon and the mail had just arrived. Grandfather Jiro could be seen already seated at the table holding opened what looked like an official government letter. He motioned the other family members to take their seats. Grandmother Keiko was the last to sit down carrying a large bowl of steamed rice from the kitchen. Grandfather Jiro led the customary short prayer before the meal. As he put a couple of pieces of gyozas (fried dumplings) on his plate, he looked around the table and said:

"I don't know any other way to say this except to simply tell all of you that we face difficult times ahead. I received this letter from the government this

morning ordering us to make immediate preparations to move to a Relocation Center in Manzanar, California. We are a security risk to the country now according to them."

Everyone around the table had a blank stare on the faces, unable to say anything, looking more sad than surprised. They had suspected for some time that this day was going to come as rumors had been circulating in the community since the Pearl Harbor attack. The constant barrage of news over the radio and hometown paper articles covering the forced relocation of *"enemy aliens"* around the country hasn't exactly been kept secret from the public either. Anyhow, what seemed like a minute or more of silence was quickly broken by Diego's mother, Kazume, breaking the silence:

"Why is our loyalty in question? We're loyal Americans. Or is it because we look different from them?"

Grandma nodded to express approval while at the same time wiping tears from her eyes with her kitchen apron. Diego, looked somewhat surprised to hear her mother readily express her opinion. She had never done that before. That's not how women were brought up in a typical Japanese household. His mother sounded anxious or upset, so he thought. Just then, Ryosaku also took his turn to speak:

"You all know that I was brought up in the old country. But I am confused too. Are we being sent away because of our race? Or is it because Japan attacked America without warning and for that we are being punished?"

Grandfather Jiro slowly put his miso soup aside and looked in Diego's direction, expecting his grandson to speak up. But Diego looked as bewildered as his grandfather, never having heard other members of the family openly express their minds like that before. His grandmother Keiko was still wiping the tears from her face when his grandfather Jiro quietly asked:

"Don't you have any opinion about all this, Diego? I had expected you to be more upset than anyone else in the family."

"I am, grandfather, but not to the same degree as Mother and the others, I guess",

he replied.

"Maybe it's because I'm no longer surprised by the written evacuation orders. We have all known for some time now that this day was coming. A few weeks ago, you told us that Reverend Tomonaga had told you and others in the congregation of the impending forced relocation of Japanese citizens and Americans of Japanese ancestry living in America."

With the others at the table nodding in agreement, Grandfather Jiro said:

"Yes, it's true. The Reverend is a highly respected member of our community. He knows influential people who have contacts outside official government channels. Of course, he had asked me and a few other parishioners to keep the matter to ourselves until it became public."

"What happens if we disobey the order, father",

asked Kasume as she poured another round of tea for everyone?

"I don't think we have a choice in the matter, daughter."

"Couldn't we just ignore the evacuation orders, Uncle",

asked Ryosaku?

"If we did, we would be forcibly removed by the authorities and suffer the consequences. I know what you're thinking. How much worse can it get? We've been told to move out of our homes and leave everything we have behind. But I suppose that compared to

other families, we're fortunate to have Diego's other grandparents to look after our farm while we're away."

"Do you know how long that will be, grandfather?"

Diego was now looking more subdued, while everyone else held their breath and waited for grandfather Jiro to respond to Diego's question. Grandfather Jiro heaved a sigh and simply said:

"I don't know, Diego",

his head held low and eyes staring at his miso soup bowl. Grandmother Keiko sensed the rising depressed mood at the table. She placed her diminutive arthritic right hand on her husband's somber face and abjectly suggested that everyone finish their dinner before their food got cold.

It had been very difficult for the residents of the tightly-knit Japanese community of Salinas to accept what they had just been asked to do - uproot their lives and just leave. There was anger and bitterness among them. Some were in denial and couldn't believe that President Roosevelt would even seriously consider issuing such an order. They had read in newspapers about the treatment and expulsion of Jews in Germany but dismissed the notion that anything similar could actually happen in America.

* * *

For the majority of Japanese-Americans, evacuation took place without incident. There were only a few cases of recorded active resistance. A U.S. Army World War I veteran, Hideo Murata, committed suicide at a local hotel rather than be evacuated. In another case,

Minoru Yasui challenged the government's actions in court. After the Japanese attacked Pearl Harbor, he volunteered for military service, only to be rejected because of his Japanese ancestry. An attorney by profession, he stated that citizens have the duty to challenge unconstitutional regulations, after deliberately violating the curfew law of his native Portland, Oregon.

Gordon Hirabayashi, a student at the University of Washington, deliberately violated the curfew for Japanese Americans and disregarded the evacuation orders. He claimed that the government has violated the 5th amendment by restricting the freedom of innocent Japanese Americans.

There was also Fred Korematsu who changed his name, altered his facial features, and went into hiding, but was later found and arrested for remaining in a restricted area. Mr.

Korematsu later claimed in court that the government could not imprison a group of people based solely on ancestry. They all lost their cases.

Yasui spent several months in jail and was then sent to the Minidoka Relocation Center. Hirabayashi spent time in jail and several months at a Federal prison in Arizona, while Korematsu was sent to the Topaz Relocation Center.

Diego's family was consumed with preparations for their impending departure since receiving official relocation orders in late March, 1942. But, as bad as things already were then, they had no clue that their situation was about to go from bad to worse! The Watsonville Register-Pajaronian had counted them among the American citizens of Japanese ancestry, numbering 3,586 in the Monterey Bay area, who were told that they would soon be temporarily confined in the Salinas Rodeo Grounds Reception Center.

A month earlier, Grandfather Jiro, despite being Issei or first generation, joined the Japanese-American Citizens' League (JACL) comprised primarily of Nisei or second-generation Japanese-Americans who were born in the United States. As a respected community elder from Salinas, he was invited to a three-day session in San Francisco to arrange for evacuation of Japanese nationals to *"reception centers"* to be set up by the Western Defense Command. Following the conference, all of Monterey County's Japanese - Americans were ordered to report to the Salinas rodeo grounds on April 27, 1942, without charges, trial, or establishment of guilt, by Lt. General John L. Dewitt, Western Defense Commander.

There wasn't much time for Diego's family to put its affairs in order before evacuation day.

Fortunately, they could count on their neighbors, the Bautistas, to look after the farm. Ryosako, had worked on the family farm together with Cesar Bautista since they were kids, harvesting the seasonal fruit and vegetable crops. Cesar had been Ryosako's friend for as long as Diego could remember. Grandfather Jiro introduced him to his future bride who was the daughter of a fellow Issei immigrant from Japan. In all the years they were neighbors, they could always count on each other when times were tough.

The two families got together for potluck dinner the weekend after learning of the evacuation order from the government. Sunday dinner was something the two families had done on numerous occasions in the past; each side bringing their favorite family dishes. However, the festive nature of past gatherings was absent this time.

As they sat down to eat, Grandfather Jiro led the usual prayer thanking God for the bountiful meal they were about to partake. Grandmother Keiko reminded the family of the numerous times the Bautistas have prepared the delicious Filipino dishes for other family gatherings such as Diego's baptism or when they had dinner over at the Bautista farm. It brought a bit of a smile to everyone's faces, although they knew that it would probably a long time before they would all see each other again.

Diego's grandparents on his father's side, the Cisneros, had also offered to look after the farm until they returned home after the war, no matter how long it took. But they were an elderly couple and lived farther away. They understood why it was better for the Bautista family look after the family farm. Diego's family considered themselves fortunate compared to many of their neighbors and friends in the same predicament. But that didn't lessen the pain and betrayal everyone felt from being forcibly evicted from their homes, for no other reason than that they were Japanese-Americans.

Diego had locked himself in his room all day long when he learned that he could not take the family dog, Kashmir, to the relocation center with them. He had raised her since she was a puppy. Half German-shepherd and half Labrador retriever, the two of them used to spend a lot of time together wading at the knee-deep creek running through the farm property. He left his room only after getting a phone call from his Argentine grandfather who promised to take good care of his dog while the family was away. The entire episode left him with a deep emotional scar all his life.

IX - Isolation

"A little rebellion, now and then, is a good thing. ... It is a medicine necessary for the sound health of government."

Thomas Jefferson

In November 1941, President Franklin Roosevelt received a secret report on the West Coast Japanese-Americans by Curtis B. Munson, a well-to-do Chicago businessman who gathered intelligence under the guise of being a government official. In his report, Munson concluded that most of the Japanese-Americans were loyal to the United States and that many would have become citizens if they had been allowed to do so. Moreover, the report stated that most of the few disloyal Japanese- Americans hoped that "by remaining quiet they could avoid concentration camps or irresponsible mobs." However, Munson also noted that the West Coast was vulnerable to sabotage, since dams, bridges, harbors, and power stations were unguarded.

Munson wrote "There are still Japanese in the United States who will tie dynamite around their waist and make a human bomb out of themselves. We grant this, but today they are few." Response to the report by Army Intelligence, although never sent to Roosevelt after the confusion following Pearl Harbor, argued that "widespread sabotage by Japanese is not expected ... identification of dangerous Japanese on the West Coast is reasonably complete. The first evacuation under the auspices of the Army began March 24 on Bainbridge Island near Seattle, and was repeated all along the West Coast.

In all, 108 "Civilian Exclusion Orders" were issued, each designed to affect around 1,000 people. After initial notification, residents were given six days in which to dispose of nearly all their possessions, packing only "that which can be carried by the family or the individual" including bedding, toilet articles, clothing and eating utensils. The government was willing to store or ship some possessions "at the sole risk of the owner," but many did not trust that option. Most families sold their property and possessions for ridiculously small sums, while others trusted friends and neighbors to look after their properties.

* * *

Diego vividly remembered that fateful day in late April 1942, when he and his family found themselves boarding a chartered bus to the hastily contrived reception center, formerly the rodeo grounds in Salinas, after reporting to collection points near their home. They fared better than other evacuees, whose family members never arrived at the various assembly centers together. In such cases, the family head was usually picked up by the FBI at his home or on his way to work and interrogated for days, before being released without having ever been charged of a crime.

Grandfather Jiro had gone on ahead of the family a few days earlier to accompany Rev. Tomonaga and a small group of Monterey community elders. They had attended the JACL conference in San Francisco and were the first volunteers to arrive at the reception centers. He was on hand that morning to greet his family upon their arrival. Diego's mother, saw him in the reception area as they were about to get in the registration line to join the other evacuees.

"It's good to see you, father",

she said, bowing at the same time to show her respect.

"Welcome, welcome everyone; I'm glad you've all arrived safely."

The remaining family members also bowed their heads, a customary practice in most Asian societies influenced by the teachings of the Chinese philosopher, Confucius, centuries earlier.

"I was a worried. With so many people expected this morning, I was afraid I would miss all of you in the crowd. Come, let's have some tea first. Then, I'll show you our new residence before you register",

pointing to the tables in the waiting room behind the reception area.

"Mother and I will get the tea and join you", Kazume replied.

Grandmother Keiko tagged along to get the tea while Ryosako and Diego grabbed the family's belongings and headed to the waiting area. A few minutes later they were all having freshly brewed hot green tea. Grandfather Jiro had just begun describing their temporary shelter for the next few months before they're transferred later to a permanent relocation center.

"Each of you will receive a number as you are registered by the employment service. Our family will reside in barracks furnished with cots, together with five other families.

These Centers were primarily established to register evacuees like us and to determine our work experience before moving us to permanent locations for the duration of the war. In the interim time, we'll have to do our best to maintain the normal life we had before the evacuation."

In reality, the atmosphere in the assembly centers was tense. Many of the evacuees were demoralized, convinced that America would never accept them as full-fledged Americans. Some Nisei who had been very patriotic became very bitter and sometimes pro-Japanese.

Former Japanese students of Watsonville held graduation exercises at the Center. Thirty high school and six elementary diplomas were taken over to former local students by school authorities. In addition to awarding of diplomas, several received gold star seals for membership in the scholarship federation. Most tried to do everything possible to make living conditions better, organizing newsletters and dances and planting victory gardens.

Nearly a fifth of the occupants at the assembly center had jobs around the camp, but the decision was made that no evacuees should be paid more than an Army private, which was then $21 per month. Initially, unskilled laborers were paid $8 per month, skilled laborers $12, and professionals, $16. These were later raised to $12, $16, and $19, respectively. Evacuees worked as cooks, mechanics, teachers, doctors, clerks, and police.

Living conditions were chaotic and squalid. Existing buildings were used and supplemented with temporary army looking barracks, 20 x 100-foot buildings divided into five rooms. Families were crowded into small apartments, measuring 20 x 20 feet. These barracks were originally designed for temporary use by soldiers, not families with small children or elderly people. Privacy was next to non-existent, with communal lavatories and mess halls. Shortages of food, other material and deplorable sanitation were common at many of the centers. The walls were also thin in these barracks. The evacuees fixed up their assigned living quarters as best they could with salvaged lumber and other supplies that they could find, in an attempt to make them more livable.

Some opportunities for leaving the assembly centers were available. California educators tried to allow college-age nisei to attend school outside of the prohibited area. Many colleges refused to accept them, but around 4,300 students were eventually released from the assembly and relocation centers to attend school. The war had created a massive labor shortage, so the WCCA also agreed to allow seasonal agricultural leave for those they deemed loyal. Over 1,000 evacuees were granted temporary leave to harvest cotton, potatoes, and sugar beets.

Although they knew that their stay at the Assembly Center was to last only two to three months, the uncertainty of what lay ahead had begun to take its toll on Diego's family. At the farm, despite the daily chores each had to do, they had privacy to look forward to at the end of the day. Grandfather Jiro missed the early evening stroll through the rows of apples and peach trees on the edge of the farm property. Grandmother Keiko and Diego's mother, Kazume, longed for the fully stocked kitchen where they prepared home-cooked family meals, while Ryosako missed reading alone in his room.

One evening during dinner at the communal mess hall, the family had found themselves seated next to old acquaintances from Salinas. The initial pleasantries and warm hugs soon turned into a lively discussion of their living conditions and the wrong that had been done to them as law abiding citizens and alien residents. Diego listened attentively. Rev. Tomonaga sounded worried when he said:

"It's so nice to see my congregation gathered together for Sunday service. We don't have the proper facility to accommodate everyone under the same roof here; the dining hall is too small and so I have to schedule the congregation in different shifts. It's just not the same; when I'm delivering God's message to my parishioners nowadays, I see the anxiety in their faces."

* * *

Just when Diego was getting settled in his daily routine at the Salinas assembly center, he learned that his grandfather had to leave them again. Like the advance party of fellow evacuees, he also led a few months earlier in making ready their assembly center, he now had to repeat the same process at their final camp destination, the Manzanar Relocation Center. Grandpa told him that the authorities had informed them that evacuees at assembly centers which had only pit latrines, or which presented a fire hazard had first priority for transfer to the Relocation Centers. He added that evacuees would be sent to the relocation center with the climate most similar to their home, and each relocation center would have a balance of urban and rural settlers. Diego didn't really care one way or the other. He just wanted to move on to a better place.

To reduce the diversion of soldiers from combat, a civilian organization, the War Relocation Authority (WRA), was created on March 19, 1942. Once the military made the decision to relocate Japanese Americans in masse, this civilian agency was left to figure out how to implement this policy. Milton S. Eisenhower, then an official of the Department of Agriculture, was chosen to head the WRA. Eisenhower initially hoped that many of the evacuees, especially citizens, could be resettled quickly. He expected that evacuees could be either directly released from the assembly centers and sent back to civilian life, or sent to small unguarded subsistence farms. However, after meeting with the governors and other officials from ten western states, Eisenhower realized that anti-Japanese racism was not confined to California.

No governor wanted any Japanese in their state, and if any came, they wanted them kept under guard. The common feeling was expressed by one of the governors:

> *"If these people are dangerous on the Pacific Coast, they will be dangerous here!"*

But their chief concern was that the Japanese would settle in their states and never leave, especially once the war was over. However, at a meeting with local sugar beet growers on the same day, a different view prevailed. Desperate for labor, the Utah Farm Bureau, while not fond of their new neighbors allowed them to work at their farms.

Eisenhower was forced to accept the idea of keeping both the Issei and Nisei in camps for the duration of the war. The idea of incarcerating innocent people bothered him so much, however, that he resigned in June 1942. He recommended his successor, Dillon S. Myer, but advised Myer to take the position only "if you can do the job and sleep at night". The evacuees were transferred from the assembly centers to the relocation camps by train; this mass movement was carefully choreographed to avoid interrupting major troop movements. The transfer process lasted from early March to October 30, 1942. Following the transfer to the relocation centers, all but two of the assembly centers were turned over to various Army agencies or the U.S.

Forest Service. Diego's family found themselves at the Manzanar relocation center.

X - Duty and Country

"There is a quote about racism,
that says it is man's greatest threat,
for it includes a maximum of hatred
for a minimum of reason."

Ed Graney, Las Vegas Review-Journal, Sept. 6, 2010, page 1C

Most Japanese-Americans who fought in World War II were Nisei, Japanese-Americans born in the United States. Shortly, after the Japanese attack on Pearl Harbor on December 7, 1941, Japanese-American men were initially categorized as 4C, enemy alien. Therefore, they were not subject to the draft. In Hawaii, martial law was declared. A large portion of the population was of Japanese descent, 150,000 out of 400,000 people in 1937, and internment was deemed not practical, mostly for economic reasons. Curfews and blackouts were imposed.

If the government had interned the Japanese-Americans and immigrants in Hawaii, the economy would have not have survived. More than 16,000 Nisei served in the Pacific and in Asia, mainly in intelligence and translation, performing invaluable and dangerous tasks. Not only were there normal risks of combat duty, they risked certain death if captured by the Japanese.

Nisei women also served with distinction in the Women Army Corps, as nurses, and for the Red Cross. Although they were permitted to volunteer to fight, Americans of Japanese ancestry were generally forbidden to fight in combat in the Pacific Theater. No such limitations were placed on Americans of German or Italian ancestry who fought against the Axis Powers in the European Theater, mostly due to practicality, as there were many more German and Italian Americans than Japanese-Americans.

Ultimately, more Japanese-Americans from the mainland would make up a large part of the 14,000 men who eventually served in the ranks of the 442nd Regiment. The combined 100th and 442nd became the most decorated regiment in American history, with 18,143 individual decorations and 9,486 casualties in a regiment with an authorized strength of 4,000 men. Both units fought in Italy and France.

* * *

As diplomatic tensions with Japan increased in 1941, even before the Japanese attacked on Pearl Harbor, the War Department Military Intelligence Division (MID) quietly turned to its Nisei soldiers to train a carefully selected few for special duty as interpreters and translators. Several officers, who had studied Japanese in Tokyo in the 1930s and assigned to Fourth Army at the Presidio of San Francisco, had selected sixty students from among the roughly 1,300 Nisei from the western states, who had been enlisted through Selective Service.

It was, however, on the morning of December 7, that reality set in as the students slowly awoke in their hangar barracks at Crissy Field on the Presidio grounds. Five weeks had passed since classes began and they had fallen into a routine. Sunday was their day off, so they had no reason to hurry. Some skipped breakfast to sleep late. The quiet was broken when they learned that Japan bombed Pearl Harbor.

America was now at war. The military and naval forces of Imperial Japan ranged at will throughout the Pacific, capturing the colonial possessions of Britain, France, the Netherlands, and the United States. Singapore, the linchpin of British defenses in the Far East, fell on February 15, 1942. On 23 February, President Franklin D. Roosevelt gave his first wartime *"fireside chat"* to the nation and recalled the Continental Army's dark days at Valley Forge. On the same day, as if to underscore the threat, a Japanese submarine shelled an oil refinery at Santa Barbara, California.

Nisei men deemed proficient enough in the Japanese language joined the Military Intelligence Service (MIS) to serve as translators, interpreters and spies in the Pacific, as well as in the China Burma India Theater. They were sent to the MIS Language School at Camp Savage, Minnesota to develop their language skills and receive training in military intelligence. Among them was Dye Ogata, who enlisted at Helena, Montana, in February 1942. He had studied in Japan from 1938 to 1940 and spoke excellent Japanese.

Another was Frank Tadakazu Hachiya, a 21-year-old college student from Hood River, Oregon, who was inducted on January 7, 1942. Hachiya was born and raised in Oregon. When his father inherited the family farm in Japan, his parents took him there and enrolled him in the local schools. When his father brought him back to Oregon in February 1940, his mother and younger brother stayed behind in Japan. Hachiya completed high school and attended college.

In the autumn of 1941, he wrote a freshman essay in which he expressed the belief that living in Japan for four years had done him a lot of good. He expressed his appreciation of America and love of one's country. He didn't mean to say that he didn't like Japan, but he will also never get so that he liked her as well as America. As he was born and reared here, he said that he was an American, although he was born of Japanese parents.

* * *

General MacArthur arrived in Australia in March 1942 to establish his new command, the Southwest Pacific Area. His chief intelligence officer, Brig. Gen. Charles A. Willoughby, began building a joint U.S.-Australian intelligence architecture that would support MacArthur's plans to halt the Japanese in New Guinea, drive them back, and eventually liberate the Philippines. The following month, the first Nisei language teams were committed to forward units. In the autumn, the US Army I Corps headquarters arrived in Australia under the command of Maj. Gen. Robert L. Eichelberger, followed by a unit of fourteen Nisei which arrived in November led by M.Sgt. Arthur K. Ushiro. Each one could read, speak, and write the Japanese language

In June 1942, Japanese language classes also began for 160 Nisei and thirty Caucasian students stationed in Australia. Eighteen Nisei instructors: eight civilians and ten enlisted men, taught the classes using the curriculum first developed at Crissy Field in the Presidio in San Francisco, based on the Naganuma readers.

The first graduates from Crissy Field convinced their Caucasian officers of their loyalty and effectiveness. The Military

Intelligence Service (MIS) Nisei and their Caucasian officers in turn convinced the War Department leaders, the Office of War Information, the War Relocation Authority, and finally President Roosevelt, of the value of allowing Nisei to serve their country. The first graduates fought alongside American and Australian soldiers and marines, using their language skills to provide combat intelligence to front-line commanders on Guadalcanal and New Guinea. They faced harsh battlefield conditions to lift the veil of ignorance that had plagued Allied commanders in the early months of the war.

Many of the early Nisei were also *"Kibei"*, having spent several years living in and attending school in Japan. Their knowledge of the Japanese language, as well as the culture and people, was very useful. Once Allied soldiers saw the value of capturing prisoners, they brought them in by the hundreds. These prisoners, treated with compassion, willingly gave their Nisei interrogators an astonishing amount of precious information.

Captured documents proved even more valuable. The Nisei used these documents to re-create the workings of the Japanese armed forces in a way no other form of intelligence could. Before the war most Americans regarded the Japanese language as notoriously difficult to learn, almost a secret weapon in itself. For most Nisei, it was not that much easier either. However, based on the three-year Naganuma program that the U.S. Embassy in Tokyo had used before the war, the MIS Language School at Camp Savage, Minnesota successfully improvised a curriculum crammed into six months. Its key feature was intensive study.

The Military Intelligence Service Language School (MISLS) in Minnesota was initially established in San Francisco and later moved in

1942 for national security reasons. Its mission was to teach the Japanese language to American soldiers. This skill could then be used to translate captured documentation and aid the American war effort.

In addition to language instruction, special topics ranged from Japanese culture and history to military terminology. School officials tried to balance military training with the language instruction. Conditioning marches across the Minnesota countryside were also part of the curriculum. The school added special instruction in prisoner of war interrogation, given the primary mission of the school and its requirement by commanders in the field.

At first the instructors recommended harsh and aggressive interrogation techniques. However, the school subsequently changed its approach. Later, it became practical to place more emphasis on compassion and kind treatment as that tended to work better from experience gained in the aftermath of the early battles fought in the Pacific theater

The MISLS recruited students from the Assembly and Relocation Centers with the following characteristics: a fair amount of fluency in the spoken Japanese; possession of an elementary knowledge of written Japanese, preferably having the capacity of reading newspapers; a good scholastic background in English and Japanese. The best candidate students usually were *"Chu-gakko"* or middle school graduates with subsequent secondary American schooling.

Nisei internees at Manzanar were interviewed; however, it could not have come at a worse time. During that period, the atmosphere in the camps had just moved from initial shock at the forced relocation to seething anger at the indefinite incarceration. Hostility and resistance appeared in the form of threats and violence against suspected informants and supporters of the camp administration. The recruiters often conducted interviews at night so potential recruits could evade watchful eyes. Volunteers inside some camps were threatened or beaten. Some Issei parents were so angered at the thought of their sons' volunteering to fight against Japan that they disowned them. To make matters worse, rumors spread that the War Department was using Japanese-speaking Nisei as spies inside the camps.

Recruiters managed to interview 439 Nisei at all of the camps and eventually selected 66 for language training. Some volunteered for the MIS language training primarily to escape camp.

> *"To be perfectly honest about it, I felt I was in a rut and just decaying in camp",*

Shoso Nomura recalled of his months in Gila River:

> *"It wasn't a normal society like, as you expect just to be able to go into business or further your education. Those opportunities were all lost."*

He volunteered for MIS in November, 1942.

* * *

It was still early morning at the Manzanar Relocation Center when Diego hastily departed for the long cross-country trip by train for Camp Savage, together with the other volunteers. The bus took them to the train depot. They barely had time to say goodbye to their families and friends.

Although shivering from the cold that late autumn morning, Grandfather Jiro remained stoic. He held his grandson's hands, while his grandmother gave him a huge hug. However, his mother, Kazume, made no pretense to hold back her tears and gave Diego a long embrace, followed by quick short kisses to his forehead. She told him to be a good soldier and be proud of his Japanese-American heritage. His cousin, Ryosako, bowed to him. Diego returned the bow and then firmly shook his hand. Ryosako was like a brother to him and he told him how much he would miss his companionship.

The new recruits arrived two and a half days later at Camp Savage in July 1942. They boarded the shuttle bus at the train station which had just unloaded several of the camp's administrators residing in town. As soon as *"roll call"* was completed, they were issued their basic uniform of khaki pants and hat. That was about it; no stripes or anything else. Technically, they were all Buck privates in rank. Then they were shown to their quarters.

The living conditions were not that much different from those at the relocation center, but no one complained. Sure, winter was coming and it was cold. The barracks had the familiar three pot-belly stoves with the coal inside. When the first snow fell, all of the guys from Hawaii ran out to touch the snow and played around in it like a bunch of kids. They've never seen snow before.

Training at Camp Savage was accelerated to produce translators urgently needed at the front. The Kibei instructors were mostly graduates of Japanese universities and had spent part of their youth actually residing in Japan. The students studied Japanese military textbooks from 8 AM to 4 PM every day, focusing on military terminology or heigo. The classes were divided according to the students' proficiency in Japanese. In Diego's case, although he was fluent in Japanese, he was not picked for the top *"all college grads"* class, because he had no college education, unlike several of his classmates who had either obtained their college education in Japan or graduated from American Universities. He had just completed high school when the Japan attacked Pearl Harbor and that interrupted his plans to attend college.

It didn't take long for him to make friends at Camp Savage. Most of his classmates were from Hawaii and were easy going. However, they were mindful first of the school's mission, and they all took their studies seriously. They were all stuck together for eight months of intensive training. In no time at all, they developed an *"esprit de corps"* within their ranks. In a letter to his family barely a week after his arrival, Diego wrote about a typical day of a student:

> *"We had reveille formation every morning followed by breakfast at the mess hall. We march everywhere it seemed: to classes, to lunch, then march back to classes, marched back to barracks. Day*

classes are over by four in the afternoon and then we're given a two-hour break to shower and march to retreat formation, have our evening meal, march back to classrooms for evening study, and back to barracks.

Sandwiched in between the daytime activities, we somehow managed to find some brief moments of respite which gave us just enough time for a quick trip to the latrine, Post Exchange, or Post Office. Also, from 8 to 10 at night, we were pretty much left alone to our own time. Saturday mornings were reserved for weekly examinations. Our only extended free time to ourselves was on Saturday afternoons and Sunday.

Our instructors do not cut any slack for anyone. They do not tolerate student excuses or inefficiency on the plea that

Japanese is a very difficult language. Added to the military and academic discipline, we are constantly reminded of our cultural heritage wherein Japanese families place a high value on education and students respect, honor, and obey their teachers.

Strangely enough though, we also have a few Caucasian students recruited from the military ranks who are fluent in Japanese. We heard that they either served as military attaches in Japan before the war or were former college students who had majored in Oriental studies. But there is also rumor in the Camp that they have been mingled among us to learn Japanese well enough so that the Army could be sure we were translating, interrogating and reporting accurately, and not deceiving our intelligence people with false information.

I guess that as Nisei we are still viewed with some suspicion and not entirely trusted. The government is not taking any chances and they really mean business."

Without exception, all of the students at Camp Savage, including those with college degrees found the intensive course study to be very demanding of their time. Despite the long hours already spent in daytime classroom study, they still had to devote additional study time at night. Many of them would stay up so late studying that *"special watches"* were alternately posted to turn off latrine lights and make sure that they all went to bed and got, at least, a few hours of sleep. They remained under constant pressure to achieve high academic performance. After lights-out, a *"duty officer"* patrolled the latrines to prevent the students from staying up all night to cram for exams. Many did anyway.

One of them was Diego's bunk mate, Arce Takahashi. Because he was also born and raised on the West Coast, it seemed natural that the two became good friends in school. Arce was recruited from Camp Tule, another relocation center in California. They were an odd-looking pair, physically that is. Diego, whose father was from Argentina was taller and had Spanish features. On the other hand, Arce took more after his mother who was from the Philippines, shorter in height and darker in complexion, resembling more the recruits from Hawaii.

Arce's family lived in Klamath Falls in southern Oregon, just north of the California border before the war. Like his buddy Diego, Arce was a high school graduate, whereas "down the line" in their Section 5 class, two of their older classmates finished college in Japan and another two graduated from the University of Hawaii. There were also several classmates who never finished high school. That didn't seem to be a problem among the general student body because as far as everyone was concerned, they were all in the same boat at Camp Savage. So, everybody broke their okole (behind) to study. *"Bakatare"* was the favorite expression of the student body, whose collective goal was to complete its stint and ship out Japanese translators to help win the war in the Pacific.

As friends at the school, Diego and Arce often talked about their families. On one occasion, Arce asked Diego what he thought about the war in general and how it affected his life and that of his immediate family. Diego thought long and hard. He was hesitant to talk about it. There wasn't much privacy inside the barracks that late Sunday afternoon; a number of their fellow recruits were within an earshot of them, busy shining their shoes.

"A lot of the guys think that we're here to prove our loyalty to America. What do you think ', asked Arce?

"I'm not going to argue with that, but I think there's a lot more to it than the guys are willing to admit in public. Deep down, there has to be more",

replied Diego.

"What are you saying?"

"Well, I think that it really is more personal when you get right down to it. There is pride, anger and a strong desire to be treated just like your average American. They're just tired of being looked upon as second class citizens."

"Sure, although I've never quite thought of it that way. I'm just as proud as

everyone else about my heritage. The anger part is something I never really felt. If anything, I was angrier at the Japs for what happened at Pearl Harbor. They pulled off a sneak attack; they didn't declare war against the United States first. That's not fair!

I could go on and on, but that's all in the past now. What's important is to keep in mind that we have to get the job done and win the war."

"Choto mate, Arce; I didn't mean to get you all riled up. We've got another hour or so before we head out for chow."

The two young recruits burst into laughter, drawing several of their buddies next to them to inquire about their lively discussion. Yama occupied a top bunk bed directly across from the one Diego had.

"What did you mean exactly by the anger part that you mentioned earlier",

Yama asked?

"I was really referring to the type of anger felt by our friends and neighbors back at the Centers who decided not to join us here. They chose to demonstrate their resentment against America by refusing to sign those loyalty papers or documents that we did, remember? They were sent to Camp Tule, because they were considered high risk",

replied Diego.

"Yeah, I know some of them because my family has been at Camp Tule since it opened", Arce added.

"Do you guys think they did the right thing", asked Yama?

"Who's to say? My grandfather always used to often tell us: 'To each his own'. I guess it's a decision an individual has to make on his own. We're all here in language school because we thought we could do our part to help win the war, although we've been treated like second classes citizens. Personally, I just want to prove that I'm an American like everyone else who was born here. Sure, I know we look different from most Americans, but that shouldn't matter. I know that sounds naive but that's just the way I feel."

"I'm with you there, Diego", replied Arce.

"Me too", Yama added.

"Let's go and get some chow, but let's keep this conversation to ourselves. You never know who might disagree with us and we could get in serious trouble."

The conversation continued at the mess hall, but was more subdued in tone, out of consideration for fellow diners. Diego mentioned being raised near Salinas and was initially relocated with his family at the Salinas Rodeo grounds. Arce heard from another student that after the Japanese-Americans were transferred to the relocation centers, the vacated Salinas rodeo grounds housed a newly formed segregated US Army Filipino regiment. He also said that because of the strict anti-miscegenation laws in effect on the west coast, many of those Filipino men married into other non-white ethnic groups. Among the most popular group to choose from were Japanese women, the daughters of Issei immigrant farmers.

Miguel Ignacio, Secretary of the Filipino American community of San Francisco, called attention to American-born Japanese women, citizens of the United States, who had Filipino husbands and Filipino-Japanese children who were U.S. citizens by birth. Despite the efforts of the American Civil Liberties Union, the US government ordered the women and children to spend the duration of the war in the internment camps. Many of these Filipino husbands went on to serve in the 1st and 2nd Filipino Regiments, defending the nation whose racist policies held their families' hostage.

The War Department already had several segregated units for African Americans and Puerto Ricans. The Office of War Information saw propaganda value in having combat units of different nationalities. In 1942, it organized the 1st Filipino Infantry in California as well as battalion-size units of Norwegians, Austrians, and Greeks.

* * *

In Minnesota, the Nisei were pleased to find that local civilians viewed them simply as American soldiers far from home. On Saturdays, generous locals waited outside the gates to Camp Savage and as the Nisei left post on weekend pass, they invited them home to dinner. The Twin Cities offered all the attractions of a Midwestern metropolitan area for their off-duty time, even a few Chinese restaurants that served familiar fare. On weekends, hundreds of Nisei descended on Minneapolis-St. Paul to enjoy the Red Cross, YMCA, movie theaters and restaurants.

In Minneapolis, there was a serviceman center downtown. And right next to it, there were two Chinese restaurants. Nanking was the name of the one Diego frequented with his buddies, since there was no Japanese food to be found in the area. Come Sunday evening, a bus from the camp came around and took them all back to their quarters. Also, with Minnesota being dairy country, Diego and his fellow recruits had all the fresh milk they could drink as well as fresh eggs in the morning for breakfast. On one occasion, they were given extended leave and so they took the time off to visit New York City.

* * *

After completing their language course, Diego's outfit was sent to Fort Blanding in Florida for sixteen weeks of basic infantry training. However, due to the urgent need for more interpreters and translators at the front, their training was accelerated and cut in half to eight weeks. But they still had to complete the same volume of war zone course work. One way to do this was to reduce the time spent marching from one training area to another. Instead of marching, troops were trucked to their destinations and back.

By now Diego had become somewhat accustomed to the daily routine of military life. The months spent in language school at Camp Savage had prepared him for the more rigorous and physically demanding pace of war time basic training at Fort Blanding, Florida and the jungle training to follow on Oahu in Hawaii before shipping out to the Pacific. As he told his family back at the Manzanar relocation center in one of his latter letters.

"We had more of the same military training we were taught at Camp Savage; you go through the formality of saluting your superiors, military courtesy and all. In the morning, we stood at attention while in formation during flag raising ceremony. At sunset, we lower the flag during retreat formation. In between, we drill and drill some more.

There is no more language training; instead, we do regular infantry training like in how to shoot the rifle, how to shoot the machine gun, how to throw hand grenades, how to dig foxholes, and so on. Training can get rough at times though. Unlike Minnesota, this part of Florida is sandy and there are lots of snakes including rattlesnakes, coral snakes. The coral snake is beautiful, but you avoid it because it is poisonous."

For Diego, the best thing about Fort Blanding was that he was there with the same guys who attended language school with him at Camp Savage. The camaraderie hadn't changed. They were a great group of guys he thought; they all got along together.

During weekday breaks in their schedule or after attending church services on Sundays, one of their favorite activities was to hone in their martial arts training in Aikido. Although Diego had already trained with a few of them back in language school, but the rigorous language curriculum at Camp Savage limited their practice. There had more relatively free time at Camp Blanding in that they no longer had to cram for language exams.

Diego initially learned about Aikido, an offshoot of Jujitsu and later Judo, from his cousin Ryosako back at the farm in Salinas before the war broke out. One day, during *"open mat"* training, Yama turned to the group in attendance and said:

> *"I think I can speak for everyone present that we don't understand why Aikido emphasizes restraint in harming someone's attacker, so that both the attacker and the receiver or defender are unharmed."*

Everyone nodded their heads in agreement.

"Precisely; let me explain what I believe Sensei Ueshiba wanted most to impart about Aikido,"

replied Diego.

"What, more lecture! When are you going to show us some techniques so we can defend ourselves against those Japanese banzai charges",

jokingly exclaimed Arce! Diego and the rest of the unit couldn't help laughing and at the same time, ignored Arce's remark.

"OK, let me demonstrate a few basic moves to illustrate the emphasis on restraint. Usually, when you are attacked by someone, it is almost always accompanied by a commitment of energy

intended to harm you. The attack is dynamic, not static. Our initial response in Aikido is to redirect or deflect that energy rather than block it or meet it head on with an equal or stronger opposing force, which is the norm with other forms of martial arts, like Karate, for instance.

In its most basic form, the defender or "Nage" has to first move aside or blend to avoid the attack. The nage can blend or step outside, inside or sideways of the uke's or attacker's stance depending on the nature or type of attack, whether he uses weapons or not.

At the same time, he executes the blend, he also uses an atemi of "distraction" such as a strike to the opponent's body to take his balance. Above all, however, the defender has to simultaneously move his "center" too, to accomplish this. This is important because by causing your opponent to be "out of balance" the successful completion of the Aikido technique in use is facilitated."

"You guys got it?"

Diego was met with blank stares from his audience. Some were nodding their heads as if to convey that they fully understood what he had said. But he knew better; the nod meant that they thought they grasped what had just been explained. The truth is that they didn't at all. So, he proceeded to physically demonstrate a popular aikido technique.

"Let me show you what I mean. Arce, stand and face me as if you were throwing a 'right hook' at my face. Do not jab; instead, throw me a punch like you mean it but in slow motion, for demonstration purposes."

"Like this?"

as Arce slowly threw a right hook.

"Yes, so as your opponent attacks, one defensive technique is to step forward with your left foot deep to his left side, deflect his right-hand punch in the same direction it was moving with your left hand. Then extend your right hand in a semi-circular fashion to strike him in the face or neck to take him off balance. At the same time step forward with your right foot to knock him down. This technique is called 'Iriminage'."

Afterwards, Diego demonstrated the complete movement again, this time at a faster pace, putting Arce flat on his back in less than two seconds. Of course, he took care not to slam him too hard on the mat. The class gasped at the speed, efficiency and effectiveness with which Diego dispatched his attacker.

More Aikido lessons in hand techniques plus the use of weapons such as the *"jo"* or wooden pole and the *"bokken"* or wooden sword, were held during the remaining weeks at Fort Blanding. Diego had succeeded in convincing his fellow recruits of the value of this new form of martial arts, whose focus is more defensive in nature.

* * *

It was war time and the US Army was not taking any shortcuts where training of the troops was concerned. More specialized training was in store for Diego and the rest of his outfit before they deployed overseas. The early battles in the Pacific had been disastrous for the US and its allies. Any stereotype of the Japanese soldier as being an inferior warrior was quickly dismissed.

With lessons learned, the US Army proceeded to ship troops like Diego and his friends to Oahu in Hawaii for jungle training.

After all the time spent in language school at Camp Savage in Minnesota, followed by basic infantry training at Fort Blanding in Florida, they found themselves facing more gruel hours of hard work to complete. However, on the bright side, Diego noticed how much happier most of the guys were to be back in Hawaii. Who wouldn't be? After all, they were at home, he thought!

Acclimating himself to his new surroundings, Hawaii proved to be a challenge although he was called a *"haole"*, having been born on the mainland. He had to frequently remind his buddies that unlike the majority of them, he was born and raised in California. He found himself one rainy weekend morning after breakfast, comparing experiences with Jerome Oba, another fellow Californian in his platoon.

"Since I was a kid, I've always heard my parents refer to Hawaii as paradise; now I'm sure they were pulling my leg. Don't you agree with me, Diego?"

"Sure, I understand,"

replied Diego while laughing at the same time at Jerome nostalgic comment.

"It's been raining continuously all week and when it's not raining, it's windy. The Army must have done a lot of research just to find this particular spot in the valley so they could say that we trained under the harshest jungle-like conditions possible."

Diego continued to laugh at Jerome's remarks. He knew him well enough to know that he was just blowing steam after the fifteen-mile forced march through the jungle the day before.

"I heard on the radio this morning that the forecast for next week is dry weather. We could use a break from all the rain, buddy."

"I can't argue with you there, Jerome. But, remember the last time it didn't rain? We had river-crossing training, where it was shallow sandy bottom first; deeper water which rose almost up to our neck came next. Then, it was pure mud on the other side, where we practiced hand-to-hand combat drills."

It was Jerome's turn to laugh. It was so loud that a few of the other guys in their unit, who were just returning from the Post Exchange heard them and joined in the conversation. Yama was quick to say:

"You got that right, brother. Right after we got back to our barracks, we scrubbed the mud off our uniforms and hung them out to dry. They didn't dry overnight because of the humidity. It wasn't until the winds came the following day that they completely dried. Lucky for us, we always kept on hand an extra set of fatigues to wear."

"Don't forget all the extra gear we have to carry in combat as language specialists. Each of us has to find some way to tote three pocket dictionaries. As a team in the field we have fourteen additional dictionaries of kanji characters and compounds, nautical terms, aeronautical terms, military terms, Japanese surnames and first names, and a copy of Webster's. We're also expected to carry a portable

typewriter, stationary, rulers, paper clips, pencils, pens, staplers, magnifying glasses, and other office supplies. That's a lot of extra baggage to be carrying into battle."

Just then, their platoon training leader, Sergeant Torres, showed up from nowhere. He was a short stocky dark man who wore his Army stripes with pride. He said:

"Men, I congratulate all of you for successfully completing your training. You have performed well and I believe you are ready to face the enemy in the field. I'm happy to extend to you an invitation from the local Filipino-Hawaiian community to a 'lechon' or roast pig fiesta, before you join the fight in the Pacific and retake Bataan. 'Tayo na' he shouted, which translated to 'let's

go', in Tagalog, the national language of the Philippines".

The entire platoon jumped and cheered Sgt. Torres. They were not going to dine on canned spam on their last day in Hawaii.

Diego made quite an impression on Sergeant Torres during one of the hand-to-hand combat training classes held. When asked to defend himself armed only with a bamboo stick against an overhead frontal *'katana'* or sword attack, Diego's favorite aikido *"Iriminage"* technique kicked in from muscle memory. He side stepped to his left, and raised his bamboo stick to the right side of his body, *"deflecting"* his attacker's sword, took his opponent's balance by moving his center and then raising his bamboo rod again to his left in a circular fashion before striking him with his full weight to bear in the neck, with the intent of cutting off his head.

Diego's platoon learned upon arrival in Hawaii that Sergeant Torres was one of the lucky ones to leave Bataan, the last bastion of defense in the Philippines, shortly before it surrendered to the invading Japanese army. He was pulled from the front line to join Philippine President Manuel Quezon, who escaped from the Philippines aboard an American submarine bound for the United States. Because of his expertise with the *"Filipino bolo"*, a machete like weapon, Sgt. Torres was dropped off in Hawaii to help train American troops in jungle survival. Every man in Diego's outfit respected Sgt. Torres as a combat veteran; they looked up to him as a war hero and a decent human being.

XI - The Enemy

"We are all travelling through history together, that you are not only living your own life but the life of your times."

Laurens van der Post

Proudly wearing the gold and blue colors of Sweden painted on her sides, the former luxury liner Gripsholm was loaded at her pier in New York harbor just a few hours earlier. She was well underway, with land no longer in sight and carrying 1330 Japanese civilians to be exchanged for 1500 Western Hemisphere nationals who were interned in the Asia when the war broke out. This was to be her second mission. She was first chartered from the Swedish American Line by the United States Government in 1942 and was also used as an exchange vessel.

The liner was going to Rio de Janeiro, Brazil, and Montevideo, Uruguay first to pick up other Japanese civilians, before sailing on to the port of exchange of Mormugao in Portuguese India, arriving there on or about October 15, 1943. From there, the Japanese liner Teia Maru, which is scheduled to arrive at the same time, will exchange 1500 Americans, Canadians and other Western Hemisphere nationals aboard. The Gripsholm was also carrying American and Canadian Red Cross supplies, consisting of medicines, concentrated foods, vitamins, and blood plasma, which were intended for distribution to American and other western hemisphere nationals left behind in Japanese controlled territories. To assure her safe conduct as a diplomatic vessel, the belligerent governments had the word "Diplomat" lettered prominently on her side as the liner was travelling without a convoy. At night, she will be brilliantly lighted to show her identity as a diplomatic vessel.

Like the Gripsholm, the Teia Maru shared a colorful sailing history. Originally christened M.S. Aramis, she was built as a passenger-cargo ship for Messageries-Maritimes in 1932. Her appearance was unusual in the fact that her funnels were square-shaped. In the 1930s, she saw passenger service on Messageries-Maritimes' Marseilles-Far East route. From 1939 to 1942, she was used as an Allied armed merchant cruiser. In April, 1942, she was seized by the Japanese in Saigon and was renamed Teia Maru. She was used as a diplomatic exchange and repatriation vessel. Later, she was used to transport Allied prisoners of war. In August 1944, Teia Maru was torpedoed and sunk by an American submarine off Luzon, Philippines.

* * *

On Sept. 2, 1943, Diego boarded the MS Gripsholm together with Japanese civilians and left New York bound for Mormugoa, Goa on the Indian subcontinent. They were to be exchanged for Americans and Canadians returning home from captivity in Japan and other Asian occupied countries. Despite the ongoing conflict, the US

State Department had successfully concluded negotiations for their repatriation, mostly Japanese men, who had sent their families home in accordance with the prewar advice of the State Department. However, those who were seriously ill and those *"primo"* special cases appointed by the State Department or Swiss Consul General were also given preference.

As the ship's horn blew announcing its imminent departure, Diego stood on the ship's promenade wondering what fate had in store for him in the months and perhaps years to come. No one knew how long the war would last and his job required him to remain in Japan indefinitely. Knowing that he could be staying with relatives in Tokyo temporarily until he meets his *"mission contacts"* gave him some small measure of comfort. He had a safety net and would not be entirely left on his own, he thought.

He was given a new identity by his superiors before he left the Military Intelligence Service Language School (MISLS) in Minnesota for this special assignment. Would he make it back home when the war ended, he asked himself? As he glanced around at the other passengers milling about the deck, snapping last minute pictures of the city skyline and the distant Statue of Liberty guarding the harbor, he heard someone asked him if he wouldn't mind taking their picture. It was the sweetest, almost angelic voice, he had ever heard in his young adult life. He quickly dispelled any further somber thoughts of the dangerous assignment that lay ahead. His mind raced to think that such an enchanting voice could only come from a woman of rare beauty. He was not to be disappointed. When he turned around in the direction of the voice he heard, he could barely manage a simple smile at the sight of wondrous beauty before him. He thought, surely this is what Homer meant when he described his legendary *"Helen of Troy"* as:

"the face that launched a thousand ships."

"Gomen nasai (excuse me), would you mind taking our picture",

the young lady asked, bowing in deference to Japan's male dominated culture? She pointed to her family while at the same time handing him a brand-new Brownie camera.

"Hai (yes), certainly."

Diego began taking photos. His prompt response was not to go unrewarded. She introduced herself as Midori Chiba and that she was travelling with her parents and younger sister. Bowing in the direction of Midori's family, Diego introduced himself as Yukata Fukuyama (his undercover identity) and that he was travelling alone. The family began to head back to their cabin, but not until Midori once more smiled at Diego and said:

"Perhaps you can join my family later at dinner time?"

"Doomo arigato (thank you), I shall look forward to it,"

he replied. He was thrilled at the prospect of seeing Midori again. He had just experienced an emotion like no other before, and wondered if this is what people meant when they say that *"it was love at first sight"*. Elated, he decided to celebrate his luck and have a drink in the ship's main salon before heading back to his cabin to finish unpacking.

It was already getting dark outside by the time Diego decided that he had enough beer. The cool ocean air coming through the open porthole to his side added a bit of discomfort. He certainly didn't want to appear intoxicated and give Midori's family the wrong impression of himself during dinner. His cabin was on the lower level, windowless and reserved for couples and single travelers, while families and VIPs were billeted on the promenade deck. Still, he was reluctant to leave his cozy seat at the bar. He didn't exactly relish the idea of staying for any length of time in his cramped quarters, but compared to the facilities back at Manzanar in California, it was luxurious. Anyhow, it was a place for him to sleep at night. He was already entertaining plans to spent as much time as possible with Midori during the long voyage to Japan.

Diego's quarters were small; a cot, side table and wash stand. He didn’t have a porthole window. The room gave him a claustrophobic feeling. He shared a bathroom with a bachelor, Nari San, in the adjoining cabin. Nari San was from Tokyo. After showering, he put on a clean shirt and a smart fitting blazer. He was waiting for a steward to come around with the ship's customary dinner bell announcement, when he decided to take a moment to go over the ship's itinerary and its various ports of call during the first leg of the journey.

A short time later, Diego found himself about to enter the main dining area to dine with Midori's family. He noticed that the other passengers seemed to have found their way to the dining hall without any difficulty at all. He was telling Nari San about how much of an appetite he had after an exhausting day boarding and stowing away his belongings in his cabin.

At the ship's banquet hall, both men were impressed at the efficiency with which the Captain and the ship's crew went about their duties. No animosity was shown to the passengers, perhaps because the staff was entirely Swedish. They dressed for dinner just like it was peacetime.

Nari San was returning to his wife and two daughters in Tokyo. He was almost finished with medical school in New York when the war broke out. But tonight, there was to be no talk of regrets or what might have been. The two men finally entered the chandeliered dining hall, its tables covered with white laced satin cloth, and crystal glasses gleaming back at them. Tuxedoed crew members were waiting to host their first shipboard dinner. Each person or family had been assigned a table for the length of the voyage. On the first night dinner aboard, they were all whisked to their assigned tables, promptly seated and served hors d' oeuvres and refreshments. A small string quartet was playing classical music.

It didn't take long before Diego noticed Midori's family already seated and ordering refreshments. Midori's father recognized him from afar and waived his hand, motioning him in their direction. He was about to join Nari San at his table when a steward asked him for his assigned table number. He was surprised to find that it was the same as Midori's family, a *“lucky seven”*. Midori's father spoke first:

> *"I'm glad you could join us, Fukuyama San. I hope you don't mind, but I had arranged to have you seated with us at the request of my daughter".*

> *"I couldn't be more pleased, Sir",*

as he bowed to the elderly gentleman and the other family members at the table.

> *"We're having wine with dinner; would you like some as well?"*

Midori interjected, visibly happy to see Diego again.

"Perhaps Fukuyama San would prefer something different to drink first before dinner",

Midori's mother asked?

"Wine would be just fine,"

he replied. Midori's father said that they probably didn't have any quality sake on board.

Dinner was served on time and was not lacking for its gourmet entrees and fine wines. With the exception of steamed rice, nothing remotely Japanese was on the menu. Neutral Sweden did not seem to have any shortages nor appeared to experience any severe rationing due to the war. Roast beef, and filet of sole were the main choices. Iron-seared salmon fettuccine alfredo, Cornish game hens glazed with honey and mustard seeds, marinated sirloin salad, asparagus soup with quail eggs and caviar.

Midori wrinkled her nose at the caviar. Conversation remained general: no one wanted to talk about their reason for being on the ship.

After dinner, Diego accompanied the family for a short stroll on the deck. He noticed that Midori's parents seemed genuinely tired, so he bade the family *"Oyasumi nasai"* or good night and went back to his cabin. The steward had made up his cot and placed fresh towels on the washstand and in the tiny bathroom. The ship was rocking gently and he fervently hoped that he would not get seasick during the long voyage. He put on his pajamas and robe and went to sleep.

* * *

The M.S. Gripsholm finally arrived in Rio de Janeiro, Brazil, and after a brief stopover sailed on to Montevideo, Uruguay to pick up more Japanese passengers. She then crossed the southern Atlantic and entered Port Elizabeth in darkness at night, through mined waters, to procure fresh water and food. On 16 October 1943, she arrived at Mormugao carrying 1,340 Japanese officials, businessmen, others and their families. The first leg of the journey to Portuguese Goa from New York had taken 44 days to complete.

On 19 October 1943, the exchange of repatriates began. Allied passengers left from the bow of Teia Maru and entered the Gripsholm via the stern gangway. The Teia Maru was carrying 1,525 passengers: 1,270 were Americans, 120 from Canada, 15 Chileans, several British, Panamanians, Spanish, Portuguese, Cubans, Argentines, and nationals from other South and Central American countries. The largest contingent of repatriates, about 975, was from China.

At the same time, the Japanese left from the bow of the Gripsholm and entered the stern of Teia Maru. A line of boxcars screened the two lines from each other. The exchange took 91 minutes. Approximately 48,760 Red Cross relief supply parcels for Allied POWS and internees in Singapore, Manila and Japan were also transferred from the Gripsholm and loaded aboard Teia Maru. Two days later, on 21 Oct. 1943, the Teia Maru departed Mormugao for Yokohama via Singapore and Manila. She arrived in Yokohama on 14 Nov. 1943.

For Diego, there wasn't a lot of time to bid long farewells on that cold, but sunny autumn morning when the Teia Maru arrived in Yokohama, her final port-of-call. He barely had time to extend his best wishes to everyone he had met on his journey. He had promised Midori that he would stay in touch with her during a private moment together after dinner on their last night aboard. He worried about her future. Confident of the superior resources in men and materials America and her Allies possessed, Diego was sure that it would only be a matter of time before Japan capitulated. He waved a final goodbye to Midori and her family as he stepped off the gang plank. They were soon out of sight altogether.

He was one of the first passengers to leave the ship. An aide to the ship's Captain had handed him a note earlier that military security men were waiting for him to disembark. As he proceeded to leave the docks, carrying a gift parcel on one hand and his luggage on the other, he noticed two uniformed men approaching him. Quick introductions followed before Diego was ordered to accompany them to the Yokohama-eki, a major interchange railway station in the Nishi-ku District. Aboard the train, he learned that he was being taken to the Kempeitai headquarters. It was next to the Dai-Ichi Insurance Company building overlooking the East Gardens in downtown Tokyo, a short ninety-minute train ride despite war time travel restrictions.

The main lobby at the Kempeitai headquarters was dimly lit, a precaution taken to ward against the incessant bombings made by American bombers during night raids over the city. Diego was led to a small back office where he waited to meet his interviewer, Section chief interrogator, Major Hachiro Ohashi. The two junior officers who met Diego in Yokohama left the room. Diego stood at attention and bowed. Major Ohashi spoke fluent English.

> *"You've had a long journey. May I offer you some tea? Let me tell you why I had you brought here."*

Without uttering a word, Diego sat down and drank his tea while the Major continued talking:

"My staff here has been anxiously awaiting your arrival since you left New York aboard the M.S. Gripsholm. We've done a background investigation on you. Of course, your fellow passengers on your voyage have also been very helpful. Your command of the English language is excellent and will prove invaluable in our interrogation of suspected enemy spies and captured Allied prisoners. The Kempeitai needs individuals with your qualifications now. I didn't want you to be taken by the Army or Navy and be assigned frontline duty overseas.

Like you, I lived in the United States when I was a young man, long before we were involved in this conflict with America. My mother, Helene Rosenthal, was Jewish from Brooklyn, New York. She made the best lox and bagels in the world! Being Japanese my father loved fish, especially salmon. My family returned to Japan at the outset of the Great Depression. Do you have any questions? Are you prepared to go to work right away? Your training will be intensive. You are going to a prisoner of war camp up north near the town of Misawa in Aomori prefecture."

"Yes, Sir, I look forward to my assignment and serving my Emperor. Will I have time to visit my family here in Tokyo before I report for training? I'll be staying with my grandfather",

Diego asked?

"Certainly, I'm sure that your relatives will be delighted to see you as well. We paid them a brief visit not long after your departure from New York; they were most helpful in our investigation into your

background. A few days with them will not cause any serious delay in your schedule. I wish you every success in our organization. The two officers who accompanied you here will provide you details regarding transportation to your next duty station."

Diego stood at attention and leaned forward as he bowed once more and shook hands with the Major, who quickly turned around and left. He remained standing while he waited for the two officers, he met earlier to complete his briefing.

* * *

It was already late in the evening when Diego was driven to his grandfather house in the Shinjuku section of Tokyo. The Kempeitai officers who had been with him all day were privy to a private vehicle. As the country's secret police, gasoline rationing did not apply to them.

Diego had intended to ride the street car, even if it meant making a couple of transfers along the way. However, with the evening *"blackout"* in effect in most areas of the city, he was happy to accept the ride. He had never met his maternal grandfather Takeo before. There was joy and a sigh of relief on the faces of both men when they did. It didn't seem that long ago when the same elderly man bade farewell to Diego's cousin Ryosako:

> *"I'm overjoyed to meet at long last, my sister's grandson. You are taller than your cousin, Ryosaku."*

> *"I'm very glad to meet you too, grandfather",*

Diego answered back.

> *"Come in and make yourself at home; you must be tired after your long trip. I*

had expected you earlier but after I saw from the window the government vehicle you rode in, I was certain you were met by the Kempeitai when your ship arrived. I recognized the uniform of the military police too. They paid me a couple of visits, making inquiries about your past while you were in-route. Would you like some tea?"

"Are you are living alone, grandfather?"

"Yes; I'm capable of taking care of myself, but I don't really cook much. I have found it less troublesome and cheaper to order most of my meals from food stalls nearby. Your grandmother passed away not long after our son was killed in China early in the war. She was never quite the same after our son died. We had his ashes interred in the Chokoji

Temple cemetery in Nagaoka, Niigata Prefecture. Did you know that Admiral Yamamoto comes from there and is a relative of your grandmother?"

"Yes, she did. She often spoke of her family from Nagaoka. I know she would like to go back there for a visit after the war. My mother said she would accompany her because she has never been to Japan."

"The war can't last much longer, Diego. Since Admiral Yamamoto's death, and the frequent aerial bombings by the Americans, the local population has realized that Japan is going to lose the war. There is nothing the officials can do to conceal that from the people.

The civilians in the city are barely getting by with their meager food rations.

There are persistent rumors that Japanese soldiers overseas are not faring much better either, according to returning wounded veterans. The Kempeitai is doing everything it can, of course, to suppress this information because it's bad for morale."

"Did the Kempeitai officers ask you a lot of question about me, grandfather? After you told them what you knew about me and our family, did they seem convinced that you told them truth",

asked Diego?

"I'm confident that you passed their investigation. They would have never asked you to join their organization otherwise. They were very thorough. They interviewed me here and at their headquarters on more than one occasion.

The fact that the war has not been going well for the Japanese people may have also helped you case.

The Kempeitai needs officers who are familiar with Western culture and the English language. They collect valuable intelligence from captured Allied prisoners in order to prepare adequate defenses for the forthcoming invasion of the homeland. Of course, you will be learning more about these matters soon enough when you join their ranks. When will you be reporting for duty?"

"I'm expected at my duty station next week. My training begins as soon as I get there."

"It shouldn't be that much more difficult for you since you've already been trained by the Americans to interrogate

prisoners. But be careful not to give yourself away. By that I meant that some of your colleagues may recognize certain aspects of your interrogation procedures as American in practice. I'm sure your superiors in America have warned about it. Be careful."

Just as they were about to help themselves to another cup of hot tea, they heard a knock on the door. It was the neighbor who owned the small ramen noodle shop across the street. He brought the food that Diego's grandfather had ordered earlier, anticipating Diego's arrival that evening.

The hot ramen soup was topped with green onions and bamboo; there was also grilled smelt, tofu and rice mixed in. It was a welcome site as both men had practically nothing to eat all day. The shop owner graciously accepted payment but not before apologizing for the lack of pork and eggs in the ramen soup, citing the shortages of most food items made difficult by the war. While his uncle searched for bowls and chopsticks to use, Diego tried to be more comfortable by stretching his legs on the tatami mat, away from the low table customarily used in Japan. The two men continued talking while eating their dinner.

"I shall have to get used to sitting like this for longer periods, or someone is bound to notice that I was not really raised in Japan, Grandfather."

"You probably won't have to worry about it too much, unless you find yourself in someone's home or in traditional Japanese restaurants. With the way the war is going plus your busy schedule, I don't think it will be much of a problem for you.

At the beginning of the war, when people celebrated Japan's early victories in restaurants all over the city, they naturally sat on the tatami mats for long periods. However, there is not much celebration going on anymore now. The Americans are bombing the country almost daily and they're exacting a heavy toll in lives and property."

The two men finished eating dinner. They drank the remaining hot tea and decided to call it a night.

Diego slept late into the next day. His grandfather did his best to move about quietly so he wouldn't wake him as he got ready to go out to get breakfast for both of them. Returning shortly, Diego was awakened by the aroma of the miso soup, hot rice and pickled vegetables his grandfather brought back. After breakfast, his grandfather suggested that they take in some of the popular sites around the city. It was another overcast day in Tokyo but the two of them still managed to enjoy visiting old family haunts amidst the debris and misery of war prevalent all around.

* * *

The trip by train from Tokyo had taken all night and most of the following day to reach the small town of Misawa in northern Honshu. But it felt less hurried to travel at night, avoiding the mass troop train movements during the day. A larger town, Hachinoe, lay further north, not far from Lake Ogawara, both located in Aomori prefecture.

Before the outbreak of World War II, Lake Ogawara was used by the Imperial Japanese Navy to practice for the attack on Pearl Harbor. The lake was used because it was similar in depth to Pearl Harbor. The Japanese military fashioned the hills near the shore of the lake to resemble the shapes of battleships and cruisers that were anchored in Pearl Harbor. This provided for a near realistic view for their pilots from the air who conducted low level bombing runs, dropping torpedoes into the shallow depths of the lake. This practice developed and refined the method to attack the American ships that were anchored at Pearl Harbor.

When Diego arrived at the train station in Misawa, he was met by an officer who escorted him on foot to his new post. He declined the ride to the camp after learning that it was less than a mile away, preferring to stretch his legs after being seated practically all night. The guard at the gate waved him on inside since he recognized the escorting officer. He was shown his quarters, a drab single-story building which also housed a dining area and an infirmary. Diego had noticed that the camp itself was not that large compared to the other military posts he had seen from his train window during the trip north. He saw only a few prisoners milling around the compound escorted by armed guards.

He was told that most of the prisoners were actually billeted on the outskirts of the town, in a larger encampment that had been used by the military since 1865, during the Meiji period. During that era, Misawa was a cavalry training center for the Imperial Army.

In 1870, the Emperor built a stud farm for the household cavalry in the area. There, he kept his own cavalry (Tenno Heika) until 1931, when the Sino-Japanese conflict required their use in China. Misawa remained a training center for Japanese cavalry until the Army transformed it into an air base in 1938 for their long-range bombers.

It was taken over by the Imperial Navy Air Corps in 1942 and in 1944 when facilities were built for the Kamikaze Special Attack forces.

Another historical footnote is that it is near the take-off site of the world's first non-stop trans-Pacific flight in 1931. Clyde Pangborn and Hugh Herndon took off from a gravel runway on the beach near Misawa in the aircraft known as *"Miss Veedol"* landing 41 hours later in Wenatchee, Washington.

Diego had barely had time to put away the few personal belongings he had packed for his trip, when he was hustled over to the camp Commandant's office. There, he was introduced to Colonel Miyashiro and Major Ota, his deputy. He still felt somewhat uneasy since putting on the uniform of a Kempetai officer when he left Tokyo. He hid his emotions well; he had no other choice. He was now a member of a harsh service with police jurisdiction that was exercised ruthlessly.

He was under orders to gather intelligence from Allied prisoners. The war hadn't been going well for Japan and collecting intelligence from Allied prisoners was assigned a high priority by the Kempetai. Major Ota told Diego that his training was to begin in earnest and conducted simultaneously with his duties as an interrogation officer. Two other officers: Lt. Terada and Lt. Watanabe were to join him in class. They had both been recently transferred from the Philippines, where the Japanese Army had been preparing plans to contain future landings by the US Army under General Douglas MacArthur.

* * *

In the spring of 1942, American Army commanders were begging for Japanese linguists for their units deploying to the South Pacific. Without front-line intelligence, units could only blunder into the enemy. Commanders needed intelligence specialists who could interrogate prisoners and translate documents quickly and accurately.

The Nisei learned that it was better to sort through captured documents quickly, rather than translate every one. They became adept at perusing large numbers of documents and picking out significant information that they could quickly translate into idiomatic English and correct American military terminology.

The US Army also learned that its prewar doctrine of questioning a prisoner through an interpreter was impractical. In theory, an interpreter could simply relay questions and answers between an intelligence officer and a prisoner. However, intelligence units at the regimental S-2 or division G-2 command levels seldom had time to interrogate prisoners in person. The Nisei learned to use their knowledge of Japanese culture and psychology to elicit information through indirect questioning. They discovered that compassionate treatment worked wonders. Their captives, expecting torture and death, were at first astonished, then grateful. Any recalcitrant prisoner needed only to hear that authorities would notify his family through the International Committee of the Red Cross that he had been captured alive. The implied disgrace could usually convince him to cooperate.

The Nisei also learned that American soldiers and marines needed constant reminders of the importance of bringing in prisoners and captured documents. Japanese soldiers, contrary to common belief, were worth more alive than dead. Tactical psychological warfare had great potential. In most cases, Japanese soldiers would fight to the death rather than face capture. But when the situation was clearly hopeless and the message properly communicated, at least some would respond to surrender appeals.

When the fighting was over, captured documents and interrogation reports were used to compile a history of the campaign from the

Japanese point of view. This gave American commanders unique insights into Japanese military psychology. Most important of all, the Nisei had demonstrated that they could be trusted to work near the front lines. Commanders and intelligence officers came to rely on the intelligence that only the Nisei could provide as close to the front as possible. Other Japanese linguists were too few or unskilled to provide the quality and timeliness of combat intelligence that ground commanders desperately needed.

The two Kempeitai officers who had just arrived from the Philippines were already waiting in the classroom, when Major Ota showed up with Diego in step behind him. Their battle-hardened faces showed the extreme hardships they had experienced in warfare in the Philippine jungles, despite their relatively young age. Major Ota sat the head of the small conference table opposite Diego and the other officers. With a stern look on his face, he proceeded to explain to the new recruits that:

"In territories occupied by Japan earlier in the war, the Kempeitai was actually under military jurisdiction. The Kempeitai had jurisdiction over Allied internees and prisoners, including local nationals.

It had jurisdiction even in Japan itself, on the grounds that they were responsible for enforcement of conscription laws and counter-espionage. Their civilian counterpart was the Tokubetsu Koto Keisatsu, Tokko or Special Police, which more closely resembled the Gestapo in Germany."

He added that the Navy had its own military police, the Tokkeitai, in areas under its control.

"Our officers and men are chosen for their superior intelligence, physical fitness, and they are given sweeping and arbitrary powers. As a Kempeitai you are empowered to arrest personnel of rank up to three grades greater than your own. You can arrest whoever you like and hold them indefinitely.

Anyone you charge with a crime has to prove his innocence, rather than the other way around, meaning that you have proven his guilt. We hold our own trials or martial law proceedings at which the defendant has no right to mount a defense and sometimes not even told the nature of the charges against him."

Major Ota briefly paused when he saw Diego visibly concerned at that point:

"Is there something that is not clear in what I've said? Do you have a question?"

In responding, Diego asked:

"Sir, are you saying that the Kempetai does not adhere to the concept of habeas corpus; that there is no presumption of innocence under Japanese law during wartime?"

"Sir, Lt. Watanabe and I understand you perfectly; we witnessed that in the Philippines",

added Lt. Terada. Nodding his head, Major Ota continued his briefing:

"The Kempeitai emphasizes espionage and counter-espionage techniques; foreign language study takes a back seat. For example, in the Netherlands East

Indies, the Indonesians regarded only one man in the entire Japanese military as fluent in their language. That is because we relied heavily on local interpreters in occupied territories.

In Korea and Manchuria, we recruited local nationals into our ranks owning to their ethnic and cultural similarities. However, they were permitted to reach only a maximum rank equivalent to Sergeant Major. We use native informants in other areas. Another exception is Rabaul, where informants were largely recruited from laborers from New Guinea who had no local roots. They were known as 'Kempei boys' and they were feared by local villagers.

You should know that the Kempeitai has responsibility for counter-intelligence throughout the Japanese

Empire. We have likewise taken a leading role in the Army's own espionage efforts; their system was copied from the Prussian secret service. Our organization has permanent resident agents in China and other areas, often based in brothels. We had active Kempeitai fifth columnist throughout Southeast Asia in the opening offensive of the Pacific War."

Major Ota went on to lecture about the role of the Kempeitai in Japanese society for another hour before breaking for lunch, followed by the interrogation of allied prisoners later in the afternoon. A quick lunch of rice balls and udon noodles at a roadside food stall plus the short hike back to the internment camp had seemed liked a long day already for Diego. He was still tired from the overnight trip by train from Tokyo. Anxious about his induction into the Kempeitai, he didn't get a restful sleep aboard the train at all.

The group entered a small dimly lit room with barely enough space for Major Ota, his three new recruits, and a uniformed guard. There was an allied prisoner seated on a stool with his hands manacled behind his back, a soiled, ragged blindfold loosely draped around his eyes. He smelled awful and the odor wafting up from his body made Diego wrinkle his nose. The prisoner had obviously not bathed recently and his uniform was stained with blood and urine.

Diego did notice something else odd about the prisoner. The dirty lieutenant bars were inconsistent with the faded areas of stripes on the sleeves. Was this person an officer or an enlisted man? Did it matter, he thought? Was this some sort of a test for new recruits? They were all there to gather as much information as they could from captured prisoners and interpret that intelligence to help slow down the Allied advance in the Pacific.

Major Ota veered from the proscribed regimen. He reminded the recruits that inflicting physical injury on a prisoner oftentimes only worsened a situation, as some men would say anything to stop the physical pain being inflicted on them. At times, this procedure merely fed false information to the interrogators. Personally, Major Ota preferred threats, intimidation, and limited beatings. His favorite weapon was a riding crop. He slowly raised the bent head of the prisoner with the metal-tipped end.

> *"This is Sergeant O'Donnell, men. He was captured in the Philippines two months ago. After escaping from Bataan last year, he joined the local Filipino guerillas in harassing the Japanese army in Luzon. He had been fed only minimum rations and has had little rest since his arrival here. He's yours, Lt. Watanabe; what are you going to do with him?"*

"I'd beat him with the crop and hang his hands up high. Then he would tell us everything", replied Lt. Watanabe "All right, Lt. Terada, what would you do?"

"I agree with Lt. Watanabe, Sir."

Major Ota then turned to Diego:

"And, what would you do?"

Diego thought carefully and responded:

"The prisoner is in bad shape, Sir. He's hungry, sleep-deprived and unlikely to give us any useful information in his condition. May I borrow your crop, Sir?"

Diego began to circle the prisoner at a deliberate slow pace with the crop at his side. Then, he lowered his head and whispered in his ear that he had been abandoned by his countrymen, and that no one was coming to rescue him. Completing his circle, he faced the prisoner again and without warning wacked him sharply on the side of his head with the Major's crop. The prisoner yelled out loud a muted *"kia"*, sounding like someone who has had prior martial arts training.

Obviously, Sgt. O'Donnell felt the pain from the sharp sting of the crop. Anticipating a swift kick or body attack from the stocky built prisoner, Diego backed off a few steps to a safe distance to protect himself. Then he moved toward the prisoner again and kicked the stool out from under him. Whereupon, the prisoner stood up and cursed in Spanish:

> *"Hijo de la puta; pendejo, (SOB, stupid)!"*

Diego understood exactly what the prisoner said but, pretended he didn't and ignored him. Then, he tore off his blindfold.

Sgt. O'Donnell was of Scottish and Sephardic Jewish ancestry as Diego later learned from the prisoner's personnel records. But what impressed Diego was how the prisoner subsequently bowed and apologized to everyone in the interrogation room for his rude behavior. The prisoner was offered rice and tea while Major Ota nodded in silent approval.

Later that day, Diego saw where the prisoners were housed. It was an abandoned warehouse. It was dimly lit and there were no beds for the prisoners. He assumed that they slept on mats and blankets on the raised wooden platforms along the walls, and took turns eating on the benches and tables tucked in a corner. There was one coal burning iron stove located in the center of the room. It barely kept the prisoners alive during those extreme cold winters in northern Japan.

The Kempeitai made frequent use of torture. The methods most commonly reported included suspending a suspect by his wrists in a way that partially dislocated his shoulders. Another was forcing a suspect to kneel and putting a heavy timber on his calves on which the interrogators stood, partially dislocating the victim's ankles. Other forms of torture included water-boarding, burning, and electric shock. Beatings commonly occurred and the *"Kempei"* were encouraged to be creative in their methods of both torture and threats.

Torture included kicking, beating and anything connected with physical suffering. But this method was used only when everything else had failed because it was clumsy. After torture, the interrogating officer was often switched with someone who asked questions in a sympathetic manner to obtain better results. When threats were made, they included hints of future physical discomforts, such as: torture, starvation, solitary confinement, and deprivation of sleep. Hints of future mental discomforts involved holding back certain prisoners last in cases where an exchange of prisoners took place, prohibiting them to send letters home to their families, meting out harsher punishment to some and lesser to others.

* * *

In the ensuing months, Diego had led or participated in the interrogation of so many allied prisoners that they became routine to him. But, there were some methods that stood out from the rest because of the unsavory procedures used. When he first saw an interrogator produce a small piece of wood which looked like a meat skewer and pushed it into prisoner's ear, and then tapped it in with a small hammer, he left the room in disgust.

The prisoner cried out loud having felt excruciating pain before passing out. Later, he was revived with a bucket of water. Eventually, the wound healed, but the prisoner couldn't hear with the punctured ear any longer. Interrogations at the camp were frequent and food was limited to small rations of boiled rice.

The Kempeitai were also responsible for managing prostitutes in areas occupied by the Japanese. This included registration and medical checks of prostitutes. They played a leading role in recruiting "comfort women" for official Army brothels set up throughout the conquered territories. Most of these women were recruited against their will, sometimes by being duped and sometimes by being arrested, particularly in Korea. Dutch and Australian women internees were also often pressured into prostitution to escape the terrible conditions in the internment camps.

At the peak of hostilities, the Kempeitai numbered around 11,000 in Japan, 2000 in

Korea, over 11,000 in China, almost 5000 in Manchuria, and almost 6,000 in the remaining Japanese conquered territories. Within the areas still under Kempeitai control, reports routinely came across Diego's desk which described activities conducted by the Kempeitai. They were used in training new recruits.

XII - Assimilation

"I am proud that I am an American of Japanese ancestry. I believe in this nation's ideals and traditions. I glory in her heritage. I boast of her history. I trust in her future."

Mike M. Masaoka, Staff Sergeant, 442 Regimental Combat Team, WWII

Since the last prisoners left in 1945, former prisoners and others have worked to establish Manzanar in central California, as a National Historic Site in order to preserve it for current and future generations. Its primary focus is the Japanese- American Internment era, as specified in the legislation that created the Manzanar National Historic Site.

No person of Japanese ancestry was convicted of espionage or sabotage during this period and over 25,000 of Japanese ancestry served in the U.S. armed services during World War II as translators and combatants. The 442nd Combat Team, all of Japanese ancestry, fought in Europe and had more casualties and more decorations than any other unit of its size.

The site also interprets the town of Manzanar, the ranch days, the settlement by the Owens Valley Paiute, and the role that water played in shaping the history of the Owens Valley.

After the war, the camps began closing and the internees gradually returned to their former neighborhoods and schools. Many of the returning veterans went to college. Those who had strong friendships with local families who promised to care for their land and property found their farms intact. Others lost everything. Many who used to run their own farms returned to work in the valley as migrant farm workers temporarily because there was a scarcity of labor and housing was available, but left as soon as they could find other work and unify their families. Some became tenant farmers and were successful in growing strawberries in the late 1940s and early 1950s.

Through the years, their plight received little attention from the general population or from the U.S. government for that matter. Perhaps, it was because of the shame felt by the older internees who didn't think they had not sufficiently taken care of their families, or thought they were betrayed. Some just hoped to move on and put this period in their lives behind them. Perhaps, because after World War II, the horrors of the holocaust in Germany took precedence and it happened somewhere else.

* * *

The war was still raging in the Pacific when Diego received new orders from his superiors in Tokyo. He was in bed in his quarters, drifting in and out of consciousness, thinking about his interrogation duties when the camp commander's aide came rushing in his room, almost out of breath, with a message:

"Sir: The Colonel needs to see you immediately?"

"What is going on; has something happened?"

"I don't know, Sir", the aide replied.

"The Colonel will inform you in due course, Sir."

Diego headed right away to commander's office. However, the Colonel was not in when he got there; his Sergeant said he was meeting with the camp supply officer and would be right back. He was asked to wait in his office until the Colonel returned.

He was anxious to find out why his commander officer wanted to see him, as he paced back and forth nervously, until he noticed a couple of tall shelves which held several rolls of maps and Army training manuals. He wanted something to read. While browsing through the maps and manuals, a folder tucked between two bulky binders accidentally fell on the floor along with some pictures in it. He tried to put the pictures back in the folder. But, as he was trying to pick them up, he noticed that there were post-card sized photos of Admiral Yamamoto and the famous American aviatrix, Amelia Earhart, among them.

He was startled, however, to also find a picture of a man who resembled a youthful Colonel Miyashiro, posing in front of a limousine Packard sedan with a California license plate. *"Holy crap",* he quietly muttered. Just then, Col. Miyashiro walked into the office while he was replacing the folder in the shelf.

Diego snapped to attention. The Colonel returned the salute. His uniform needed a good pressing and his dimly lit office made it somewhat difficult to read his facial expression. Kerosene lanterns did not provide good lighting but it was enough to see that the Colonel's face was flushed and Diego thought he had been drinking again. Sake at the camp was in plentiful supply locally despite wartime rice rationing. In a burst of temper, Col. Miyashiro threw Diego's orders across his desk.

> *"You must know some people in high places in Tokyo for you to receive urgent transfer orders to Argentina, Lieutenant!"*

> *"I beg your pardon, Sir; but there must be some mistake*",

replied Diego.

"I'm afraid not; I took the liberty of confirming your orders; there is no mistake. As valuable as you are to me at this post, I have no choice but to let you go. The orders came from the top. We both know the war is not going well for Japan."

"Before your orders came, I had hoped that we could both wait out the war here. You speak English very well and if you remained here at the camp, the Americans might be prone to treat us more leniently after the war. I would have placed you in charge of supervising the transfer of the prisoners to the Allies after Japan surrendered. The prisoners respect you despite being a Kempeitai officer."

"You don't have much time; you have to leave at once. I wish you good luck in

your new assignment; you have been a good officer under my command."

Colonel Miyashiro then countersigned the orders. The men saluted and bowed to each other. A stern looking junior naval officer was waiting outside the Colonel's office to escort Diego to the navy port in Aomori, an hour's drive north of the POW camp at Misawa. But first, he had to stop at his quarters to grab a few things for the journey. He took only a few personal items such as: a picture of Midori, his sweetheart, a civilian suit, a summer uniform and his government issued Type14 Nambu pistol.

On the way to Aomori, his escort told him that he was being taken to a waiting submarine, on a special mission to the Panama Canal. The crew was going to drop him off in Valparaiso, Chile first. Lots of things went through his mind as he was being briefed about his trip. It was all happening so fast. It was early summer, 1945. He knew that the war was going to be over soon and he wanted to be present at Japan's surrender. He had hoped to remain in the country a while longer with the American occupation forces. However, fate had once again intervened and whisked him off to a different direction in his life. Now, he was being reassigned to a military attaché posting at the Japanese embassy in Buenos Aires.

* * *

Diego had always loved the sea as far back as he could remember. Growing up near the ocean on the central California coast, he could recognize the scent of the Pacific and the fog that clung to its surface miles away. The waters surrounding the sub base in northern Honshu was no different, although it was 7000 miles in the opposite direction from the California coastline. This time, the Pacific crossing was going to be an entirely new experience. He was going to be submerged under water during most of the trip. He felt uneasy about boarding a submarine.

Finally, despite the icy roads and inclement weather characteristic of winter in Aomori, he arrived at his embarkation point. He promptly boarded the only submarine in port and shown to his quarters. With his personal luggage stowed away, the sub's captain wasted no time getting underway on the long voyage after a brief introduction to the crew.

> *"I'm Captain Mifune. You are aboard an I-400 class submarine aircraft carrier in-route to the Panama Canal by way of Valparaiso, Chile. We have on board with us a special passenger that is going there. That is all you need to know because our mission is top secret.*
>
> *We will be crossing the Pacific under water most of the time. We will surface*

only at night to charge the sub's batteries when no other objects are visible on the periscope and there is no full moon. We will not be stopping at any other ports. Do not worry, you will be safe. It could take a week or more to reach Valparaiso, depending on how much time we spend evading enemy surface war vessels.

We have brought enough fresh water and food to make a month's crossing and back to Japan, if necessary."

As luck would have it though, the voyage got off to a rough start with a storm approaching in their path. Captain Mifune assured them that they would be safe submerged beneath the surface, and that American warships prowling the Pacific were a greater menace.

Diego was assigned a bunk next to that of another Kempeitai agent, Lt. Pablo Igawa, who was going to the Panama Canal on a different mission. His mother was an American. He grew up in El Paso, Texas adjacent to the Mexican border and was fluent in Spanish. Diego was careful not to reveal any slightest mannerism that might make Lt. Igawa suspect that he was also raised an American.

The two agents hit it off well right from the beginning. Lt. Igawa was a likeable Texan at heart, a “straight shooter” as they say in Texas, rather than the stereotype stoical Japanese male. Understandably, there were also several navy pilots on board; the submarine had a couple of aircraft which Diego saw secured on its deck. Aboard, the first thought that crossed his mind was how cramped his quarters were, despite being told that the I-400 class was the largest submarine in the Japanese Navy. Still, he could only imagine how much smaller the space must have been for the lower ranking enlisted men.

Diego kept to himself most of the time during the trip, aside from reading a couple travel guides about South America and an occasional exchange of war stories with his bunk mate, and a few members of the crew. He frequently thought about the danger of traveling in such tight quarters with no visible easy way of escape if they came under attack.

The rationed meals of canned squid and sardines further added to his anxieties. Whatever fresh fish, fruit, vegetables and other perishables they had on board at the outset of the trip were consumed in no time at all. There was no refrigeration aboard. A crew member told Diego, they considered themselves lucky to have been issued any fresh rations at all, considering the war shortages. Diego learned about the special preference given to submarine crews due to the extreme danger they constantly faced. American submarines were constantly on patrol and every trip out to sea was for all practical purposes logged as a suicide mission.

Just as Captain Mifune said at the outset of their voyage, the passengers hardly saw daylight during the crossing, surfacing only at night to avoid being spotted by enemy aircraft or surface ships. Several of the sailors were former university students who studied astronomy before the war. They would go out on the deck whenever the submarine surfaced to gaze at the stars.

The Captain and his crew were battle-hardened sailors, having narrowly escaped numerous close calls in the past. The fact that they were still around late in the war was proof of their skill and experience in evading the enemy. Some of the crew members, however, admitted that luck also played a hand in it. It was rumored that Captain Mifune was the last remaining survivor of his class from the naval academy at Etejima, near Hiroshima.

Midway through the Pacific crossing, Diego noticed that Lt. Igawa was beginning to show stress from prolonged confinement. One evening after retiring to their cabin, the Lt. confided in Diego:

> *"I survived repeated counterattacks by American and Filipino troops on the Bataan peninsula in the Philippines. I thought then that nothing else could possibly be more terrifying. But these suffocating quarters are worse. I don't know how much more I can take."*
>
> *"I know exactly what you mean, Igawa San. I'm foremost a land creature myself; that's why, I didn't join the navy when the war broke out. Was Bataan as bad as returning veterans say it was?"*

"Intelligence didn't report all the facts; the truth is, we were beaten on Bataan. The real reason the Americans surrendered is that they ran out of food and supplies; otherwise they would have kept on fighting. The Filipino troops didn't want to surrender either; they kept attacking our lines day in and day out. They fought like samurais; we held them in high regard as soldiers.

We had to recall men on their way to Malaya and Burma back to Bataan, to replace those who were killed in the initial fighting. This angered the survivors so much that they exacted revenge on the surrendering troops. When the Americans and Filipinos surrendered, we marched them more than 60 miles to internment camps without food and water. Those who couldn't walk or simply gave up were killed where they stood.

The Filipino civilians who tried to help them suffered the same punishment. As an officer and a practitioner of the Bushido code, I tried to save as many as I could, both military and civilian. Some of my fellow officers tried to stop the senseless killings too, but there were not enough of us. Most of the others simply turned a blind eye to the atrocities that were committed. When General Yamashita, learned what had happened, he ordered an immediate stop to it".

"Do you suppose that General Yamashita's background and his strict Bushido code of honor had anything to do with halting the harsh treatment of the prisoners during the march?"

"I suppose so. As a high-ranking general officer, he was bound by the rules of the Geneva Convention regarding the treatment of prisoners of war."

"But Japan wasn't a signatory to the Geneva Convention."

"You're right, I forgot. But, duty and honor aside, he may have also been thinking that he could be held accountable for the atrocities committed in the Philippines after the war."

"Surely, after Bataan, things got a little bit better after the fighting stopped and peace was restored, didn't it?"

Lt. Igawa paused and let out a deep sigh, as if to convey he was glad that Diego had changed the focus of their conversation to the occupation of the islands by the Japanese army.

"I fell ill after the fighting on Bataan stopped; the doctors told me it wasn't malaria and that all I needed was an extended rest period. I was accompanying the troops who were guarding the prisoners when I was stricken with fever. I think I had simply been out in the hot sun too much, day after day. We were heading for the capital of San Fernando in Pampanga province; the prisoners were to board a train there to take them north to their permanent camp in a place called Cabanatuan."

"Did you end up boarding the POW train too",

asked Diego?

"No, I was taken to a small town, not far from our main route: Floridablanca, where we had a local garrison of about 300 men. I was treated at the infirmary on the outskirts of town. I was content to spend the remainder of the war there; it was peaceful and far from the guerilla fighting taking place all over the main island of Luzon. The presence of several hundred more of our men at Clark Field in the next town, Angeles, served as a deterrent against guerilla activity, I suppose. I also met a special girl in Floridablanca. Her name was Maria and her family were very kind to me. I brought them rice and canned goods whenever I was invited to dinner. She made the best banana fritters I've ever had".

"But, how did you get to meet Maria when we weren't exactly welcomed as

liberators by the Filipinos after invading their country?"

"After the Americans surrendered, we made serious efforts at community building during the early occupation. We taught the children in the local schools. In fact, that was how I met Maria; her brother-in-law was a teacher. Since I spoke English, and Spanish we got along just fine. The fact that I was grew up in Texas and my first name was Pablo also helped me earned their trust, although somewhat still guarded because I wore the Japanese Army uniform.

Overall, language was not a problem, because most Filipinos learned to speak English when they came under American rule after the Spanish-American war of 1898. I told my parents that I would return to the Philippines after the war to marry Maria."

"Did they approve of your plans to marry a foreigner",

asked Diego? The Lieutenant hesitated for a second to answer, realizing that he may have revealed too much already about his personal life or spoken out of line as a Kempetai officer.

"I think I might have had too much sake tonight; I'm feeling a bit tired now. What do you say we turn in?"

"You're right, Lieutenant It's late; we'll catch up with the rest of the story tomorrow."

He didn't want to appear surprised but, Diego did find it a bit odd to hear of the Lieutenant's plans to wed a Filipino woman. But the Lieutenant was also half American, he realized. Still, Japan remained a xenophobic nation and a lot of value was placed on the purity of their race. Marrying outsiders was considered taboo because they were brought up to think that they were superior to their rest of their Asian neighbors.

* * *

Diego basked in the clean unpolluted air and bright sunshine upon arrival in Valparaiso. He gorged on fresh bananas, mangoes and papaya available in every corner fruit stand. After a couple of days ashore, with his sea legs stabilized and a schedule to keep, he decided to push on with his mission. First, he took the bus connection to Santiago and from there the overland route bus to Buenos Aires. Along the way, he enjoyed meeting the locals virtually unaffected by the war, something which rarely came up as a subject of conversation at all.

The indigenous population was more worried about the prices of the goods they were bringing to market. The war has created shortages for just about everything as demand exceeded supply. He learned about volunteer pilots from Argentina and infantry units from Brazil fighting with the Allies in Europe. That made him feel good being an under-cover US Army intelligence officer. He was temporarily free from the atmosphere of suspicion and fear that consumed daily life at the allied prisoner of war camp at Misawa.

It was Saturday morning and the overnight bus ride from Santiago afforded him much needed sleep and rest, he could only dream about when he was holed up inside the submarine during the Pacific crossing. When he arrived in Buenos Aires, he stayed at a modest hotel on Corrientes Avenue downtown. He wanted to see the city landmarks first before reporting for duty the following Monday. The night life of tango bars and salons, asado or grilled meat restaurants and the beautiful women at every turn only confirmed the stories his Argentine grandfather had told him as a young boy. He remembered the ranch in Salinas, California his Grandfather owned, where he spent many wonderful summers.

Monday morning came sooner than Diego wanted and it was time to report for duty at the Japanese embassy. He was escorted inside by a member of the embassy staff. He couldn't believe his eyes when he was introduced to the Ambassador. It was none other than Midori's father. He was completely taken by surprise. Warm handshakes ensued, followed the customary formal bowing. Naturally, he wasted no time inquiring about Midori. Then, Diego learned that it was the Ambassador himself who had asked for his transfer to Argentina. He confided in Diego that his transfer was made possible through powerful government connections his family had with Prince Konoye, who was the Prime Minister to Emperor Hirohito before the war. Prince Konoye never wanted to go to war against America.

Diego was to serve as a non-uniformed Kempeitai officer, tasked with laying the groundwork for the Japanese version of the Nazi *"Odessa"* pipeline. Its objective was to assist former high-ranking Japanese officials to evade capture by the American Army after Japan's surrendered Although his posting was in Argentina, his mission's territory encompassed all of South America. He was told to begin the process of paving the way for senior Japanese officials who wanted to escape to South America even before Japan surrendered to the Allies. They were to eventually link up with their Nazi counterparts who had already begun filtering into Buenos Aires and farther to the south of the country, in the Alpine-styled city of Bariloche, to form the *"fourth Reich"*. Many of the former

Nazis who had escaped from Germany resettled in the neighboring countries of Uruguay and Bolivia as well.

* * *

The war in Europe continued to go bad for the Axis powers. The German war machine had suffered serious setbacks in Russia while Italy's Benito Mussolini was deposed and hanged by his own countrymen. Rumors of looted Nazi gold and precious art work being stowed aboard submarines headed for South American countries with sympathetic ties to Germany abound in Argentina's capital. It was during this time that Diego had also learned of the fate of Lt. Igawa, whose submarine continued on to the Panama Canal after dropping him off in Valparaiso. The US Navy sunk his submarine before it reached its destination. He was told that there were no survivors.

* * *

His Argentine and Japanese ancestry had served him well in life as a young Army intelligence officer during WWll. He had successfully infiltrated the dreaded Japanese Kempetai at an allied prisoner of war camp in northern Japan. When WWll ended and the cold war emerged between the United States and the Soviet Union, Diego found himself again in the service of his country in a similar job. The geographical location, people and culture may have changed, but he was still in the spy business; this time, as a CIA operative in Argentina.

Diego had no intention of waiting any longer before asking Midori to marry him. The couple both realized that it was only a matter of time before Japan surrendered after the news of Hitler's death and Germany's official surrender. Midori's family welcomed the news and began to make plans for a private wedding.

The wedding day arrived at last. Only a few members of the diplomatic circle in Buenos Aires attended the event together with the Japanese Embassy staff. For a brief time, those in attendance chose to forget the bad news they continually received, realizing that Japan had already lost the war. Nonetheless, it was a happy gathering for the bride and groom. Also, although the war had not fared well for Japan, Midori's family fortune remained intact in foreign banks and they spared no expense when it came to the wedding of their only daughter. She had waited a long time to be reunited with Diego, since they first met during her family's return trip to Japan after the Pearl Harbor attack.

* * *

With the wedding nuptials over, Diego thoughts turned to returning to California with his new bride for a short visit. He hasn't seen his family since he left the Manzanar relocation center. He was due a furlough and he had a lot of "back pay" coming for time served behind enemy lines during the war. He was eager to introduce his new bride to his old friends and relatives. Midori agreed with the idea and urged her husband to do it before he got bogged down in his new assignment. They booked passage on a liner to San Francisco as soon as their travel documents were ready.

It was a joyous reunion with both sides of his family. His mother, Kazume, and his grandmother Keiko and grandfather Jiro could not believe their eyes at seeing how he had matured to adulthood, surviving the war behind enemy lines and now a married man.

Shortly thereafter, he learned for the first time of the death of his cousin, Ryosako, who was killed in action in Italy. He was a medic with the segregated 442nd Japanese-American combat regiment and was decorated for heroism under fire. Grandmother Keiko told Diego how Ryosako often wrote in his letters that he missed his younger cousin so much and that he looked forward to seeing him again after the war. Diego was devastated when he learned of Ryosako's death. They were like brothers, inseparable before the war. The entire family wasted no time in making the three-hour trip from Salinas to the Presidio in San Francisco to visit Ryosako's grave.

His Argentine side of the family was also there to greet him home. They were just as happy to learn that he has taken up residence in Argentina, where all those stories about the *"old country"* he heard from his grandfather had originated. There was not a single dry eye among the members of his family who were present at his reunion, which lasted late into the night. Plenty of Argentine asado or grilled beef, empanadas and wine were on hand to the accompaniment of live Tango music. It was just like the old days when Diego used to spend the summers at the ranch belonging to his Argentine grandparents.

During the festivities, Midori told Diego that she felt like she was back in Buenos Aires with the atmosphere and company being so similar. His grandfather could hardly contain his joy at seeing his grandson whose mannerisms resembled so much those of his only son who died before Diego was born.

While on holiday, Diego had also noticed that his childhood acquaintances had not adjusted well in comparison to the general population. This was despite the benefits that came with the rapid suburbanization and industrialization of the post-World War II era. After the war, the United States supplied the allied countries with manufactured goods while Europe and Japan struggled to rebuild their post-war economies. Lots of jobs were available, but mostly to whites. Although agricultural and manufactured products were in high demand in the post-war torn economies of Europe and Asia, there was also a downside to the post-war economic boom.

For most of the former Japanese-American internees from the Santa Clara valley in California, land had become too expensive for farming. And many of these Nisei or second-generation Japanese-Americans had to find other employment opportunities. The sons and daughters, as well as the grandchildren of the older Japanese farmers were also reluctant to follow in the footsteps of the immigrant generation. The succeeding generations were college educated and trained in professional and technical fields. Farming was no longer the main economic form of employment within the Japanese-American community. Diego could be counted among them.

Culturally, over the years, as older Issei or first-generation Japanese-American internees died, their stories of imprisonment disappeared with them. Many of the second generation or Nisei also chose not to talk about their experiences. Midori said:

"As a native Japanese person, I can only explain it as refusal to accept what really happened."

"I'm not sure what you're trying to say."

Diego replied.

"There are two popular Japanese expressions I know to help explain what I mean. One is 'gaman,' which essentially means 'to tough it out.' The second is 'shikata ga nai,' which roughly means 'it cannot be helped; it is out of my control,

therefore accept it.' One conclusion I have come to is that this thing that happened to your parents, the incarceration, is so demeaning that they have difficulty acknowledging that it happened. It is a form of denial.

Didn't you tell me before about the incident involving the daruma doll at the camp where your parents were interned? A small piece of paper resembling the Japanese daruma doll was given to each person. The daruma is a symbol of wishes for the future, and the custom is to color one of the doll's eyes while making a wish, and then the other if the wish comes true. Everyone made a wish and pinned the small paper darumas to an 8-foot-tall replica of a guard tower. It's hard not to guess that many of you made the same wish, that for what happened here nearly five years ago to never happen again."

Diego could only ponder what Midori was really trying to communicate to him. The day's celebration with so many guests at their *"Welcome Home"* reception was still being replayed over and over in his mind.

The remainder of their trip was dotted with sightseeing tours of San Francisco's Chinatown on the city's iconic cable cars, the Palace of Fine Arts, the Marina District, and of course, the Golden Gate Bridge. Diego and Midori couldn't have made a better choice about their honeymoon destination.

* * *

Six months after their wedding, highlighted by their long-awaited trip home to visit relatives in California, Diego was ready to get back to work at his new job. The war with Japan had abruptly ended after the United States dropped two atomic bombs on Hiroshima and Nagasaki. At long last, Diego was able to reveal his true identity to Midori's family too. The US government placed no blame on Midori's family since they didn't openly support the Japanese militarists.

At his new job, Diego was recognized a *"silent hero"* for his courage and loyalty by Mr. Donovan himself, founder of the Organization of Strategic Services (OSS), the forerunner of the Central Intelligence Agency (CIA). It was only a matter of time before Diego transferred to the CIA after the OSS was dissolved.

As a CIA field operative during the postwar years, Diego kept tabs on senior Nazi officials who fled to South America. His duties also involved tracking known Japanese war criminals who might have escaped to Peru, and Bolivia. A number of these Japanese war criminals sought family connections with the first generation of

Japanese families who immigrated to those countries during the 1920s for economic reasons.

While the Japanese government during the postwar late 1940s and the 1950s was more concerned with rebuilding the country's infrastructure and economy, its embassy in Buenos Aires was preoccupied with the political upheaval of the Peron dictator led government. As a result, Diego also became involved in keeping a watchful eye on Argentina's national politics.

When General Juan Peron became President of Argentina in 1946, his populist ideology was known as Peronism. His wife Eva Peron was equally if not more popular with the masses, and also played a leading political role until her death in 1952. But censorship characterized his regime.

Between 1943 and 1946, Peron closed down 110 publications and the number of unionized workers and government programs also increased. An isolationist foreign policy was followed in an attempt to reduce the political and economic influence of other nations. Government spending increased significantly which, in turn, led to an unacceptable level of inflation.

From 1948 to early 1950, the peso lost about 70% of its value; inflation reached 50% in 1951. Those members of the government who opposed Peron were imprisoned and some of them were tortured. Many important and capable advisers were dismissed, while those who professed personal loyalty were promoted.

Inevitably, a coup, Revolución Libertadora, led by Eduardo Lonardi and supported by the Catholic Church, deposed him in 1955. He went into exile, eventually settling in Spain, which was under the dictatorship of General Franco. It was no secret to the public and the international community, that Peron welcomed former Nazi officials into Argentina. It was even rumored that the Catholic Church may have helped his government planned their escape from Europe. Buenos Aires was their point of entry into South America.

This, of course, did not go unnoticed by the CIA. After all, didn't the US government also become directly involved in bringing top Nazi rocket scientists, such as Eric Von Braun, into the United States to help kick off its fledgling rocket spaceship program? But the agency claimed that the former Nazis being hunted in South America were hardened criminals who were responsible for murdering millions of Jews and political prisoners.

In reality, Diego didn't have much of a choice. This was the new directive from Washington and his priorities had to shift with the new policy. He was told to back off from finding Japanese war criminals in the region and search for Nazis instead. Furthermore, his superiors selected him for the job because his ethnicity made him less suspicious to those he was looking for. This was the same reason he was assigned to intelligence duty as a Kempeitai officer in Japan during WWll. This didn't really bother him, professionally speaking and he accepted his new duties without any reservations.

XIII - Discovery

"Every saint has a past
and every sinner has a future."

Oscar Wilde, Irish Poet,
1854-1900

The stellar record of the Japanese Americans serving in the 442nd and in the Military Intelligence Service in Pacific Theater during World War II, helped change the minds of anti-Japanese American critics in the United States. Eventually, it resulted in easing of restrictions and the release of the 120,000 strong Japanese-American communities well before the end of the war.

However, the unit's exemplary service and numerous decorations did not change the attitudes of the general U.S. population to people of Japanese descent after World War II. Veterans were welcomed home by signs that read "No Japs Allowed" and "No Japs Wanted", denied service in shops and restaurants, and had their homes and property vandalized.

Anti-Japanese sentiment remained strong into the 1960s, but faded along with other once-common prejudices, even while remaining strong in certain circles. Conversely, the story of the 442nd provided a leading example of what was to become the controversial model minority stereotype. According to author, historian Tom Coffman, men of the 442nd dreaded returning home as second-class citizens. In Hawaii these men became involved in a peaceful movement. It has been described as the 442nd returning from the battles in Europe to the battle at home.

The movement was successful and put veterans in public office in what became known as the Revolution of 1954. The phrase "going for broke" was adopted from the 442nd's unit motto "Go for Broke", which was derived from the Hawaiian pidgin phrase used by craps shooters risking all their money in one roll of the dice.

One notable effect of 442nd's service was to help convince Congress to end its opposition towards Hawaii's statehood petition. Twice before 1959, residents of Hawaii asked to be admitted to the U.S. as the 49th state, but each time, Congress was fearful of having a co-equal state that had a majority non-white population. The exemplary record of the Japanese-Americans serving in the 442nd and the loyalty showed by the rest of Hawaii's population during World War II overcame those fears and allowed Hawaii to be admitted as the 50th.

* * *

WWll ended twenty years ago and memories of that tragic period in history are fading away. Around the world, the generation which lived through it and were fortunate enough to survive were much older now. In Argentina, the tumultuous regime of the dictator Juan Peron was finally over. A small measure of political stability had returned and the country's economy was on the mend.

Given this relatively favorable climate, Diego seriously thought about retiring from the CIA. After all, it was the early 1970s and a long successful career at the Agency had run its course, he thought. The old spy, as his family affectionately refers to him nowadays, had also raised a family and now, he longed to return home to his native California. He knows he'll miss the assignments and postings he held as a field operative but, he wasn't getting any younger and it was time to hand over the reins to a new crop of younger agents.

His last major assignment felt like it took 10 years off his life. He led agents in tracking former Nazis who used the *"ratline"*, an underground network of escape routes and support personnel created for Nazis trying to make it to South America after the war. He tried to find Klaus Barbie, Martin Bormann and other Nazi war criminals as well as lesser known Japanese war criminals who might have also escaped to South America. Emotionally, this kept him on edge all the time. It has taken its toll on his overall health. But he felt somewhat uneasy about calling it quits altogether.

There was so much left to be done and his gut feeling told him that there were still loose ends that only he could wrap up. He knew deep down, of course, that wasn't true. He has trained the other agents well and was confident they could take over his duties. It was the pride in his work and perhaps a bit of ego that made him want to cling to his job just a little bit longer. Diego was always very thorough too in whatever endeavor he undertook. Midori often reminded him that it was simply human nature to think we are indispensable. Her own father agonized over being forced to leave the Foreign Service when he reached retirement age.

Actually, this final episode of his career began earlier in the 1960s and spilled over into the 70's. At its inception, the worldwide hunt for Nazi criminals who had escaped to South America right after WWII was back in fashion. The likes of prominent Jewish Nazi hunters like Simon Wiesenthal, who was credited with bringing Adolf Eichmann to justice, brought back the horrors of the Jewish holocaust into the public eye. But for Diego, this time it involved finding just one particular Nazi official, namely: Martin Bormann, personal secretary to Adolf Hitler.

The last piece of intelligence the Mossad had on file on Bormann was that he had boarded a submarine for Panama after he left

Hitler's bunker in August 1945, when the Russian army began encircling Berlin in the final days of the war. What puzzled everyone, however, was why he never arrived in Tokyo, his final destination. This was later confirmed by Lt. Igawa, who was Diego's former bunk mate aboard the submarine which brought him to South America.

Not long after WWll, Diego learned that Lt. Igawa survived the war after all. He didn't make it back in time aboard his sub, when it left the Panama coast on its return voyage to Japan. He was captured by the local authorities while on a reconnaissance assignment inland. Fast forward a decade after Japan surrendered in 1945 and the former Lt. Igawa was now a Special Agent in the Japanese Secret Service. He stayed in touch with Diego throughout the Cold War and became Diego's *"eyes and ears"* in Tokyo. One evening at his office, Diego recalled a telephone conversation the two had:

"How was your furlough back to America? Did you take the family with you? I would have, knowing how much you enjoy spending your time off with them, according to our intelligence reports."

Laughing out loud, Diego replied.

"You're pulling my leg, because we know your budget is limited, with Japan bent on rebuilding its economy first and so on. You guys couldn't afford the resources to tail me and my family. We're still funding your agency, without the knowledge of Congress, of course. Am I right?"

Both men laughed again.

"Listen Igawa San, the agency is re-opening the Martin Bormann case. According to our latest intelligence report, he has been spotted living in quiet seclusion in a rural section of northern Bolivia. I know you reported that he was supposed to hook up with you in Panama in May, 1945. You were assigned to escort him back to Tokyo aboard the same submarine which dropped me off in Valparaiso."

Agent Igawa then asked:

"What's going on 'tomodachi' (friend)? Everyone now knows that Bormann died in Berlin after leaving Hitler's bunker, a couple of weeks before the Nazis surrendered. That's why he didn't show up to meet me in Panama. I was also supposed to bring back to Japan the latest V2 rocket technology and other

Nazi miracle weapons. Are the Israelis putting you guys up to this? I asked because they've been making inquiries over the wire here, in Tokyo too."

Diego hesitatingly responded:

"Yes, the local Mossad office is spearheading the effort and we're lending them a hand. We owe them for the assistance they provided us in finding high- profile Nazis in Europe right after the war. Help me dig up any information you can from your end about Martin Bormann. I'll see what the Mossad here in Buenos Aires has in their files on him. I'll be in touch."

It was a daunting task even for someone with Diego's experience coupled with the assistance he was getting from Agent Igawa and the Mossad office in Buenos Aires. The leads he was getting from his network of fellow veteran spies locally and abroad was not always reliable. For instance, it was rumored that Bormann eventually took another boat to Brazil where Adolf Eichmann and Joseph Mengele were thought to also be in hiding. The Mossad certainly thought that this was plausible, since financial and security support would have been readily made available to Bormann by established communities of Nazi sympathizers in the region.

The Mossad is Israel's secret intelligence service responsible for foreign intelligence collection, political action and counterterrorism. Its principal function is to conduct agent operations against the Arab nations and their official representatives and installations throughout the world. This is particularly true in Western Europe and the United States, where the national interests of the Arabs in the Near East conflict with Israeli interest. Mossad collects this intelligence for the protection of the State of Israel, Zionism and Jews in general.

The Collection Department is responsible for foreign covert operations and the processing and production of reports from clandestine sources. This component is the largest unit in Mossad. The department has offices abroad under Israeli diplomatic and nonofficial cover. It is active mainly in Europe, where it concentrates on Arab targets through third-country operations.

There is also a Psychological Warfare or Special Operations Division, in the Political Action and Liaison Directorate, which runs highly sensitive covert action operations against Arab terrorists and ex-Nazis. It also includes sabotage, paramilitary and psychological warfare projects, such as character assassination and black propaganda.

Geographically, Mossad operations abroad fall into two principal categories: those in the Near East, as a first line of defense, and those elsewhere. Mossad stations outside of the Arab areas in the Near East are generally under diplomatic cover within the embassies and consulates of Israel. There are stations in the United States, most of the European capitals, Turkey, Iran and strategic centers in Latin America, Africa and the Far East.

* * *

Diego was also hesitant to take early retirement from his job because of the persistent rumors he heard about his old wartime boss at Misawa, Col. Miyashiro. His former Kempetai superior had crept back into his life. Acting on a recent tip from the Mossad, Diego made up his mind to attend a party celebrating Hitler's birthday, 25 years after his death. The occasion was meant to be low-keyed and kept secret from the local Jewish community.

The Mossad coerced former members of Peron's intelligence apparatus to get an invitation for Diego, so he could pose as a member of the press. This would remove any suspicion of him having a direct link to the Mossad. He had attended similar gatherings in recent years in neighboring Paraguay and Brazil, but this one got all of the local intelligence units buzzing with activity. It didn't take him long to understand why. Any reservations or doubts he may have had about the reliability of local Mossad intelligence dissipated when he was asked to contact his liaison.

Diego discreetly made his way to the banquet hall after showing his credentials to the guards at the gate. He had to present them again inside the hall. Security was tight; something

Diego knew a lot about. Notwithstanding the numerous invited guests and all of the security present at the event, Diego wasn't discouraged from looking for his former boss. So, you can imagine how happy to finally spot him, mingling in the crowd.

Ironically, it was Colonel Miyashiro though who saw Diego first. The astonished Colonel was accompanied by his security detail when he approached Diego. Initially alarmed, Diego thought about leaving the scene, but it was too late. He instinctively bowed:

"Isase bure desu ne (It has been a long time)!"

The Colonel acknowledged Diego's formal greeting:

"Indeed, it has been a long time. I am surprised to see you. The war ended over

twenty years ago. I inquired about you at the Japanese embassy here in Buenos Aires after Japan surrendered. No one seemed to know who you were, much less tell me where you went. I gave up looking after a while. Your credentials show that you are working with the local newspapers; am I right?"

Quick to think on his feet, Diego responded:

"Yes, that's correct. I'm an independent reporter; I share my stories with different newspapers throughout the country, depending on their focus: political, financial or entertainment."

"And you would, I presume, want this event to be reported as a political event?"

“Any gathering of former high-ranking Nazi officials anywhere in the world, particularly in Argentina, attended by WWll colleagues from Japan is a newsworthy story, Sir”,

replied Diego.

“Ah, yes of course, and the victor writes the history books. I look forward to reading it and finding out more about the work you’re doing now,”

added the Colonel as one of his aides nudged him to move along to meet the other guests.

Once more, Diego bowed in deference to the rank his former commander presently held in the post WW II Japanese Secret Service. Judging from the size of the delegation he led, Diego couldn’t help thinking of the extent of the influence he must have had too, among the former Nazi officials present. However, he was also concerned because he knew that Col. Miyashiro would henceforth try to find out more about his job. The Colonel was adept at that doing that sort of thing.

* * *

When Diego reported his encounter with his old boss to his superiors in Washington, he learned that the CIA had the Colonel recorded as deceased. The American occupation force in Japan had captured him in Osaka several months after Japan surrendered aboard the USS Missouri in Tokyo Bay. He was hiding with associates of the Red Dragon Society, which was a high-profile criminal organization operating in Japan and other Asian countries. He was found guilty and hanged for the mistreatment and killing of POWs at Misawa. Obviously, Diego had to tell his superiors that they got the wrong man.

The photos of Col. Miyashiro taken at the event in Buenos Aires in honor of Adolf Hitler's birthday, and the physical description Diego provided convinced the top senior officials at the CIA of the error they made. The Colonel may have initially succeeded in evading capture after the war by assuming a new identity, but Diego was a credible witness, because he was at the POW camp at Misawa. He could positively identify Col. Miyashiro. Diego's Mossad contacts in Buenos Aires wasted no time in putting him directly in touch with one of their agents.

Diego suggested meeting at a small café bar in San Telmo, a quaint section of Buenos Aires frequented by locals and tourists alike for its charming shops, boutique hotels and street tango performers. In this way, he could easily get lost in the crowd if he suspected anyone tailing him.

Inside the café, Diego noticed the dining section packed with the regular lunch crowd. He wasn't surprised since he often took business associates and guests from out of town there himself. He got the usual friendly nod and *"hola"* greeting from the staff as he headed for the bar, which was practically empty except for one middle-aged bearded man enjoying a tall draft of Quilmes. He appeared to be enjoying it too, considering there were two other empty mugs of this fine Pilsen right in front of him. The Quilmes brewery was founded in 1888 in Quilmes, Buenos Aires province, by Otto Bemberg, a German immigrant.

"Mr. Weinstein",

Diego asked? When the man turned to face him, Diego was astounded and left speechless. He knew the gentleman. He was the former POW sergeant he interrogated at Misawa during the war. It was Sgt. O'Donnell in the flesh! He recognized Diego too and said:

"Holy mother of God, tell me: is it really you Lt. Sawa? You saved me from a fate worse than death at the POW camp in Misawa, remember?"

"Of course, Sergeant; how could I forget! I can't believe it; what are the odds that we would meet again after what we've both been through? I'm your Agency contact, but call me by my first name, Diego."

"I had no idea you were assigned to work with me, your surname being Weinstein. Is that a cover?"

"No, not really. I adopted my mother's maiden name when I was recruited by the Mossad in Tel Aviv after the war. My

mother's side of the family were Sephardic Jews. They were exiled to what is now Palestine during the Spanish inquisition in Spain centuries ago. Have you heard of them?"

In a sympathetic tone, Diego said:

"Yes, I have. My father's family originally came from Spain before they immigrated to Argentina in the early 1800s. I can assume that you know what persecution and suffering of a people is all about; you are a survivor".

Agent O'Donnell nodded in quiet approval:

"It's good to see you again. How can I be of service?"

The two men reminisced a bit more about their past lives and then discussed the details of their plan to eliminate Col. Miyashiro including the method, location and time period in which it was to take place. They agreed to proceed with caution until final approval from the Agency is received. The two men then separately left the bar.

At the other end of town, Colonel Miyashiro decided to extend his stay in Buenos Aires to launch his own investigation into Diego's true identity. He sought help from his contacts within the Red Dragon Society in Japan to find locally affiliated members. Inquiries were circulated in the underground throughout Argentina and Japan. Where did Diego grow up? Who were his parents? Which schools did he attend? What was his service record during the war?

It didn't take long before criminal elements succeeded in obtaining the information he was looking for. Bit by bit, information about

Diego's background began to trickle in. Colonel Miyashiro started to connect the dots when he learned where Diego resided in his youth and how he came to be fluent in Japanese, Spanish and English. But something else had been gnawing him, as far back, when they first met in Misawa during the war. He realized that it was Diego's facial trademark which convinced him that he was the same infant whom Admiral Yamamoto left with his sister in Salinas before the war.

Colonel Miyashiro recognized the *"protruding forehead"* to be a Yamamoto family trademark. It was passed on to Diego from his grandmother, who was the sister of Yamamoto's mother. He was sure, beyond any doubt, that when he drove Admiral Yamamoto to Salinas to visit his aunt, Diego was the infant who was dropped off at the farm in Salinas to be so raised by her family as one of their own.

Colonel Miyashiro felt betrayed and was enraged upon realizing that Diego was actually an American intelligence operative, disguised as a Kempeitai officer while under his command. Not one to *"let bygones be bygones"*, he immediately ordered a *"hit"* on him. Colonel Miyashiro wanted Diego assassinated in Buenos Aires and make it appear like Peron's agents were responsible. After all, the CIA had also been snooping on Peron's activities. He ordered subordinates within the Dragon Society to get rid of him. It was not a popular decision among the rank-and-file members. They thought that their activities in Argentina might be exposed or even compromised. There were whispers that the issues the Colonel had with Diego were more personal than actually mission related.

The Mossad informed Diego of the contract out on him. So, he decided to also make his move against Colonel Miyashiro while he was still in Buenos Aires. Diego secured approval from his superiors to *"eliminate"* Colonel Miyashiro as well. This came, of course, with the tacit approval of the Japanese Secret Service, when they learned that the Colonel himself had hidden his true identity and the heinous acts he committed against Allied POWs. He had become a liability to their organization and an embarrassment to U.S. and Japan relations.

To avoid any suspicion from the local authorities, mostly former agents of the Peron regime, Diego sought support from the Mossad offices in Tokyo. This helped him keep tabs on Colonel Miyashiro's Red Dragon associates residing in Japan at the same time.

On orders from headquarters in Tel Aviv, Mossad agents in Buenos Aires disguised as *"tango turistas"* succeeded in planting a bomb in Colonel Miyashiro's apartment in the upscale Palermo district of the city. Tragically, a number of innocent residents also died in the bombing. The police investigation reported that an elderly male wearing Colonel Miyashiro's clothing and shoes was found in the ruble and the case was closed.

* * *

Another decade or so went by before Diego finally decided to retire from the CIA. He wasn't getting any younger, he often told Midori. But she knew better; Diego wanted to go back to California for good this time. He left with a modest pension. The entire family returned to California, settling in Novato, north of San Francisco across the Golden Gate bridge in affluent Marin County. Initially, he rented an apartment for himself and Midori for six months while he helped his adult kids find housing for their own families. He found his boyhood town of Salinas still mostly rural.

Compared to Buenos Aires, long considered by many as the *"Paris of South America"* at the time, there was not much to do in Salinas by way of entertainment or dining options for his family.

Eventually, the family ended up buying a small bungalow in Novato, a small bedroom community in Marin County bordering Sonoma County, south on Hwy. 101. Novato was about 25 miles from San Francisco and housing there was more affordable, being farther from the city. A lot of SFPD cops resided there too for the same reason.

Novato also had a more racially diverse population than, for instance: Tiburon or Sausalito, where the wealthy lived in homes with magnificent views of the Golden Gate bridge and the city skyline across San Francisco Bay. The town itself is located between San Rafael to the south and Petaluma to the north; the latter was also known as the *"chicken capital"* of California. Diego's kids loved the area and the time they spent together, although they were also pretty much occupied with raising their own families.

Diego's son was a decorated Vietnam war veteran. He was drafted into the US Army in the mid-60s despite living abroad in Argentina. He used his GI Bill to finish college with a Bachelor's of Science degree in computer science. He worked in San Rafael for a high-tech firm as a System's Engineer. Diego's daughter resided in the next town over, Corte Madera, where she taught special education students. The family, including the grandkids regularly got together for Sunday dinner. Friends and neighbors were occasionally invited too. Diego would often remind his family that although we may not be able to choose our parents in life, we are certainly free to choose our friends. It was good advice handed down from generation to generation in his family.

To stay fit, Diego and his son took Aikido classes during the week. Diego's training in Aikido went back to his youth at the family farm in Salinas, where his cousin, Ryosako, gave him his first lessons. He continued his training with Army buddies during the war and CIA field operatives later.

He enjoyed playing golf in his retirement years. Twice a month, he would drive into the city and play a round with fellow government retirees at the Presidio. He loved the scenic views of the Golden Gate Bridge from greens which faced the Marin headlands jutting out into the vast Pacific. After the game, he'd shoot the breeze with his friends over a cold mug of draft beer. Then, he would take a sort hike to his cousin's grave at the National Veterans Cemetery a few blocks away.

During one of those golf outings, while enjoying his usual mug of cold beer at the bar, one of his friends, Robert Tyson, remarked pointing to the TV on the wall:

"A local station is showing a Japanese news broadcast of government officials in Tokyo paying homage to their war dead; isn't that frowned upon by certain groups in the US and Japan?"

"Isn't that the old Shinto shrine in downtown Tokyo",

asked Dennis Takhtalian, his Armenian friend? He had on occasion told Diego about how his countrymen were persecuted, in the hundreds of thousands, by the Turks in the past century. He added:

“I’ve been there. I was with the occupation force serving with a military police unit after the war. It’s the Yasukuni Shrine in Chiyoda. It was founded by Emperor Meiji in 1869 and commemorates those who died in service of the Japanese Empire. Enshrinement at Yasukuni signified meaning and nobility to those who died for their country. During the final days of the war, it was common for soldiers sent on kamikaze suicide missions to say that they would "meet again at Yasukuni" following their death.

The Shrine lists the names, origins, birthdates, and places of death of over a thousand war criminals, fourteen of whom are considered A-Class. They included the prime ministers and top generals from the war. You see the dilemma this presented and the controversy which naturally followed."

"That's true; it's a very sensitive subject to many who still remember the war and the numerous atrocities inflicted by Japanese troops throughout Asia, especially in China, the Philippines and Malaya. Also, who can forget the rape of Nanking and the Bataan Death March silently condoned by those war criminals",

Robert concluded, as he bought another round for everyone.

Diego was about to join in the conversation when he recognized one of the senior Japanese officials in the delegation. He stood up from his bar stool to take a closer look at the screen. Sure enough, he saw his former POW camp boss, Colonel Miyashiro himself, attending the ceremony at the Yasukuni Shrine. He could hardly contain the surprised look on his face. He was sure he had the man assassinated by the Mossad in Buenos Aires a decade earlier. Fortunately, the broadcast had ended and his golfing buddies had decided to call it a day. Diego was eager to get back home to contact his old boy network at the Agency and find out what went wrong.

* * *

It was not often that Midori or the entire family tagged along with Diego to the city. When he went to play golf at the Presidio, he usually carpooled with a couple of his friends who also lived in Marin County. But this time, the Japanese community in the Bay area was celebrating the annual Cherry Blossom festival that week. Midori wanted the family to attend the festivities because one of her relatives from Japan, who was prominent in Tokyo's political elite circle, was a guest speaker at the reception. There were, of course, Japanese dignitaries present.

The guests were all gathered in a large banquet hall at the Nikko hotel in Japan town. News crews and photographers from Japan and the local media were also present. The event made the front page of the Tokyo Daily Shimbun. It was during this time that former associates of Colonel Miyashiro in the Red Dragon Society recognized Diego in one of several photos published in the widely circulated Japanese newspaper. These were the same agents who had accompanied the Colonel to Buenos Aires more than a decade earlier and where they had also planned to assassinate Diego.

Their old boss, now an aging former WWll Kempeitai officer, had wormed his way into a senior position in the Japanese Secret Service after the war. He was thought to have died in a Mossad orchestrated apartment building bombing explosion in Buenos Aires.

Colonel Miyashiro was overjoyed to learn of Diego's whereabouts. He disclosed his findings to the ultra-nationalist Dragon Society whose powerful top leaders promptly decided to assassinate Diego, because he would be an embarrassment to Japan. Eager for revenge, the aging Colonel ordered the local San Francisco chapter to get rid of Diego for good this time.

Officially, Diego may have retired from the CIA; but he still kept in touch with his former associates at the Agency and at the Mossad. He reported back too that he had recognized Miyashiro with a group of Japanese officials making their annual visit to the Yasukuni Shinto War Shrine in Tokyo.

Clearance was also given by top CIA officials to liquidate Colonel Miyashiro in the interest of national security. Orders were passed on to the Mossad as well. They were more than happy to be given another chance to do the job. After all, they botched their first opportunity more than a decade ago in Buenos Aires. They were determined to get it right this time too. Colonel Miyashiro was killed by a sniper's bullet as he was leaving a night club in Tokyo's Shinjuku district. Ironically, it was done with the final approval coming from his superiors in the Japanese Secret Service for the good of the country.

* * *

At long last, Inspector Chavez got back the identity report he had requested from the CIA at Langley, Virginia. It was delivered around half past noon on a Friday, when the agent conveniently timed his arrival at SFPD headquarters to be less conspicuous. Most of the officers and staff were out to lunch. The Inspector recognized the type: someone a tad taller than the average man on the street, wearing a dark suit and a white shirt, spit-shined shoes, confident and composed in bearing. But, what he didn't expect was someone who was half his age. The agent introduced himself.

> *"I'm Special Agent Wells, from the FBI. You must understand the sensitive nature of what we're dealing with here, Inspector. This comes straight from the top and I've been asked to convey to you that this is matter of national security. As a senior law enforcement officer and a decorated war veteran, we trust you not to reveal this to anyone else except on one condition."*

"What is that", asked the Inspector?

"Before you break the seal, you'll need someone to witness you read the contents of the package, and also trust to keep this meeting secret. Can you get in touch with someone today?"

"I trust my partner, Sgt Lee. I can ask him to meet us here; he's home today. It's his day off", the Inspector said.

"That will be fine. I can discuss the contents in detail with both of you when he gets here. Can I help myself to some of your coffee while we wait for him to get here?"

Sgt Lee dropped everything he was doing at home when he got the call from his partner. He could tell from the tone of his voice that he was in some sort of a bind. The Inspector couldn't have been more forthcoming or direct when he asked his partner to haul his ass over to the office.

When Sgt. Lee showed up, the three men moved to the interrogation room across the hallway. It was secure and sound proofed. The Inspector wasted no time opening the package brought by Agent Wells. Its content was labeled *"Top Secret"*. He glanced around the room to make sure no one else was there except the three of them. Then he poked his head out into the hallway once more to double check that no one was in the immediate vicinity either. The Inspector's looked anxious as he removed the security label off, eager to see its contents. The Inspector broke the seal and read it out loud:

"In consultation with top CIA officials, the FBI directs you, in no uncertain terms, to drop the Presidio investigation in the interest of national security.

Japanese officials at the highest level of government insist upon it. This would avoid the national embarrassment that is certain to ensue if the public ever learned that Admiral Yamamoto had fathered a child out of wedlock with Amelia Earhart.

The victim your office has been investigating was their illegitimate son. You should also know that Amelia Earhart was spying for our government when she made the "round the world" flight that ended tragically."

Both detectives looked dumfounded. The Inspector leaned over to show Sgt. Lee the signature of the FBI Director himself. Before they could say anything, Agent Wells told the Inspector to burn the letter in his presence. With embers from the burning letter in the metal waste basket still glowing, he further stated:

“Gentlemen, your country is indebted to you both.”

He then handed Inspector Chavez his business card, which read Robert Wells, Haberdasher, a telephone number with a 703-area code and an address in Langley, Virginia. His business card seemed a bit odd, showing him posing as a proprietor of a haberdashery shop. The Inspector thought to himself: who has suits custom tailored in this country anymore except the perhaps the powerful and wealthy. But then, it was really the name that seemed to have jogged the Inspector’s memory. He asked Agent Wells:

“Any relations to Senator Shelby Wells?”

“The senior Senator is my grandfather, Sir”,

as he nodded and tipped his gray fedora hat. His black leather briefcase in hand, he departed without saying another word.

End

At a Glance - the author

Emmanuel Tiongco Santos was born in the Philippines in 1948, to a naturalized Filipino-American father who served as a combat engineer with the US Army in Europe during World War ll. A Vietnam-era veteran himself, the author enlisted in the United States Air Force in 1966. He was stationed at Misawa AB in northern Japan in 1968 until he was honorably discharged from active duty in May, 1970.

The author attended the University of California on his GI Bill and graduated with a Bachelor of Arts degree in International Relations in 1971. A long successful career in corporate America with large software companies such as: Electronic Data Systems (EDS) and Oracle followed. He began his profession as a computer programmer and quickly rose through the ranks as a systems analyst and project manager. Years later, he became a salesman "pounding the pavement, pressing the flesh and showing the flag" world-wide in commercial and government markets. He retired as Vice-President of International Sales in 1994.

Currently, he is a resident of Las Vegas, where he remains an avid golfer, a tango enthusiast and a martial arts practitioner. He also enjoys fly fishing in Utah, and ocean surf casting in central California coastal towns. He regularly trains in Aikido, Karate and Judo to stay in physical shape. In 2016, he earned his black belt in Aikido. He writes as a hobby, finding it a welcome respite from the rigors of active retirement, lol!

... the author at his home course, Paiute Golf Resort in Las Vegas, Nevada, USA.

Made in the USA
San Bernardino, CA
13 December 2018